THE
LAST
GIRL

THE
LAST
GIRL

A MYSTERY

DANNY LOPEZ

OCEANVIEW PUBLISHING
LONGBOAT KEY, FLORIDA

ISBN 978-1-60809-252-9

Published in the United States of America by Oceanview Publishing
Longboat Key, Florida
www.oceanviewpub.com

10 9 8 7 6 5 4 3 2 1

PRINTED IN THE UNITED STATES OF AMERICA

For Flor, may you rest in peace

ACKNOWLEDGMENTS

First and foremost, I'd like to thank Bob and Pat Gussin and the folks at Oceanview Publishing for taking a chance on me and Dexter Vega. I would also like to thank my wife, Lorraine, for her undying support and unflinching love. I must also thank my kids for putting up with my protracted mental absences whenever I'm in the writing "zone." Thank you all.

THE
LAST
GIRL

CHAPTER ONE

I DROVE OUT to Memories Lounge, an old hole in the wall in the shitty side of town. The place had a decent jukebox and an old Rock-Ola from the seventies that played real 45s when it was operational—a fifty-fifty chance on any given night. The walls were covered in cheap wood paneling and the ceiling tiles were black from decades of cigarette smoke. It was as good a place as any to drink cheap and forget you were unemployed and running out of money fast.

Three months had passed since the layoffs at the *Sarasota Herald*. They were trimming the fat, boosting stockholder profits. I should have seen it coming, but I was too caught up in my own ego—Dexter Vega, superstar investigative reporter. When the list of names came down the pipe in a group e-mail, I was blindsided. Almost knocked me off my goddamn chair.

Not that I'm bitter. I can take it like the best of them. I packed up my shit, waved a middle finger at the publisher, and never looked back.

Memories was never full, and that night, that early, it was almost empty. Just a table of college students and some old guy in a purple polo sitting a few stools from me. I pumped a buck in the jukebox, chose a Johnny Cash tune and Bob Dylan's *Tangled Up in Blue*. Mac, the bartender, had a ball game on the old tube televison behind the bar.

I was nursing a Corona, wondering what the fuck I was going to do with the rest of my life. I had given my blood to journalism, and it had stabbed me in the back. When my wife took off with our daughter, she cited my obsession with work as the single reason she could no longer live with me. I hated losing her. I hated losing Zoe.

Halfway through my third beer, this guy marched into Memories, parked himself between me and the old man in the purple polo. Mac gave him a nod. The man just leaned against the bar and stared at the old man.

He looked rough—two days from homeless. Had dirty blond hair and nice blue eyes. Probably mid-thirties. But life made him look older—late forties. I could smell him from where I sat. Foul. Old banana peels and Jack.

He said something to the old man. It didn't look like a conversation. He seemed like the kind who doesn't talk to you—talks at you.

I turned my attention to my own problems. My severance money was running out. Something had to give. And this summer I was supposed to get my kid. Zoe was turning seven, and I had to show her a nice time. Maybe take a short vacation, Busch Gardens or Disney. That shit wasn't cheap.

The rough guy said something to the old man with the polo. I didn't catch it, but then he raised his voice, cussed, and shoved the old man. He pulled him off the stool, threw him back. The old man dropped flat on the floor, arms out like Jesus. I stood. The rough guy pounced on the old guy. Sat on his chest and hammered him twice on the face with his fists. One-two. Then he picked him up like he was trash and shoved him against the wall. The old man bounced back from the wall to the rough guy's arms like he was made of rubber. Then the rough guy pushed him out the door toward the parking lot.

I was right behind them. I know. It was none of my business, and I'm not crazy about old people, especially after living in this town for so many years. But what was I supposed to do?

I'm not a fighter. Five-nine, a hundred sixty pounds, and totally out of shape after a three-month bender. Still, I was angry at the world. I guess I needed something to distract me from my own misery.

Outside, the rough guy had the old man folded over the hood of a beige, late model Lexus 460. He held the old man's head by a fistful of hair at the back and was slamming his face against the bodywork.

I grabbed the rough guy by the arm and threw him back. He fell on the pavement. Not so difficult, but he stood up real quick. Fucker had to be sober as a goddamn stone. He grinned at me, charged—caught me by the waist and dropped me like a pro. I saw stars. He probably would have hammered me unconscious in five seconds if Mac hadn't come out with that Louisville Slugger he keeps stashed under the bar.

The rough guy stared at him, his little blue eyes shining like lights. Then he bailed. Ran off into the dark. Gone.

Mac checked us out. Asked if we were okay, if we needed an ambulance or the cops. I was surprised to see the old man spring back to life despite his bloody nose and lip. He'd taken it good from that asshole. But suddenly, it was like it never happened. He dusted off his pants and stretched out his shirt and ran his hand over what little hair covered his head.

Mac rested the bat on his shoulder and walked back in the bar.

"Thank you." The old man had a pleasant, confident voice with a slight accent that reminded me of the Italian bartender at Caragiulos restaurant downtown.

"What was that about?"

The old man shrugged. "Beats me. People these days, eh?"

"I guess."

He wiped the blood from his lip with the back of his arm and spat. "Probably just angry he lost his job." Then he smiled. Earlier, at the bar, I would have guessed his age to be in the seventies. But when he smiled, he looked younger, could pass for sixty.

"Please," he said, "let me buy you a drink."

He took a step forward. His legs wobbled like they were made of yarn. He leaned against the Lexus for support.

"You okay?"

"Just dizzy," he said and waved his hand in a circle in front of him. "It'll pass."

"Maybe you should go home and get cleaned up." I pointed at his face. "Put some ice on that lip." It didn't look serious, but you can't ignore a split lip, blood all over his purple shirt.

He touched his face and looked at the blood in his hand. He smiled like a happy grandfather. Crazy, smiling like that after he'd had his face bashed against the hood of a fifty-thousand-dollar car.

"You live far?"

He shook his head. "On Bay Shore. Just over the Trail."

Blame the humanitarian in me. I mean, that's why I got into journalism, right? To save the goddamn world. "Come on." I pointed to my ten-year-old, beat-up Subaru. "I'll give you a ride."

His name was Nick Zavala. He lived in a slick house on the bay. It wasn't one of those new pseudo-Mediterranean McMansions with wide columns, long balconies and red tile roofs. No. His place was a single story, modern deal from the late sixties. It had class. I respected that.

"Why don't you come in and have a drink with me?" Nick said when he stepped out of the car.

"No offense," I said. "I don't swing that way."

He chuckled. "I didn't mean it like that. You helped me out of a jam. I pulled you out of a bar. I owe you one."

Don't ask. I'm not sure what I was thinking. Maybe I was done with Memories for the night. Maybe it was the old man's grin or his eyes or the fact that I was still shaking from the fracas with the rough guy because I'm not a fighter and that monster could have wiped the floor with my face.

I was suddenly very, very thirsty.

Nick's place had the looks of a bachelor pad from the early seventies: sunken living room, shag carpet, and a wall of glass that opened up to a pool. But a thick hibiscus hedge obstructed the million-dollar view of the bay. Still, you could smell the sea, and if you got on your toes and stretched your neck, I'm sure you could catch a glimpse of the ocean.

Nick excused himself and went into the bathroom. Front center, over a long white leather couch was one of those Andy Warhol Marilyn Monroe silkscreens. It was numbered and signed in pencil.

"Warhol gave it to me himself," Nick said when he came back to the living room. "It has a dedication on the back."

People talk a lot of shit. I'm a journalist. I know. But I had the feeling Nick was being straight with me. All the art in the living room had that same quality: sixties and seventies pop art you'd seen in movies and magazines. Most of the rich people in this town decorated their homes with art from one of the local craft fairs: paintings of palm trees, beach scenes, flamingos—or posters you could buy at Target. This guy had the real deal. I'm not an art expert, but I knew enough to recognize a real Jim Dine, a Robert Rauschenberg, and a Peter Max. There was even a strange assemblage by James Rosenquist at the end of the long dining room.

Nick went to the bar. "What's your poison, friend?"

"You got any tequila?"

He smiled. "I have rum."

"That'll do."

"Coke?"

"On the rocks is fine."

"No," he said. "Would you like to hit a few lines?"

I turned away from the art and walked to the bar where he was pouring me a rum and preparing himself a bourbon.

I shook my head. "Just the drink, thanks."

"Sure."

That's when I realized he was sizing me up. Measuring my game. I didn't mind. It's how it is. But I was curious: a sixty-something-year-old guy who lives in a stylish house on the bay that's gotta be worth a couple of million with an art collection that's right out of a museum is hanging out at a shit-hole bar like Memories invites me for a drink and offers me cocaine.

What. The. Fuck.

He handed me a glass and came around the bar, his own drink in his hand. He nodded to the dark sky past the hedge to the bay. "Home sweet home."

"Must be nice."

"It is. But nothing's perfect."

"You're telling me."

He took a long drink and pointed at me with his glass. "You're Dexter Vega. From the newspaper."

"Not anymore."

"I always enjoyed your work."

"Tell it to the editor," I said. But it wasn't as if I would ever go back. Even if they begged me to return, on their knees, offered me a raise—a big one—two extra weeks' vacation. Never.

"It's a shit deal, eh?" he said. "To be laid off after . . . how many years?"

"Twelve. And a half."

He raised his glass. "Their loss."

I touched his glass with mine and we drank. We moved slowly to the couch, a big white leather divan you probably couldn't even buy in this town. He sat. I remained standing. It's a better perspective when you're in a rich person's house. Always stand. Drink their booze, keep a clear perspective.

"That piece you did on the Sarasota Police covering up after their own. That was some top-notch reporting," he said.

His flattery of my work was nice, but it made me wary. I'm naturally suspicious.

"It took a while to put the pieces together," I said. "But when the puzzle was complete, it was all real clear. Besides, cops are a unique breed. They stick together. But when they smell blood, forget it. Sharks."

He nodded. "So what are you doing now?"

I raised my glass and took a long sip of rum. "Drinking."

He smiled. "Sit, please. Just for a moment."

I sat on the chair across from him. An Eames recliner. Leather. Cool and comfortable.

"I wonder if you could do something for me."

So there it was. Best friends already.

"I need someone to help me find my daughter." His expression was dead serious. His little eyes locked on mine. I didn't like it.

"Is she lost?"

"I'm not kidding, Mr. Vega. She sort of disappeared a few months ago—"

"Sort of?"

He smiled and pointed at my drink. "Need a refill?"

I looked at my glass. "Yeah, but first tell me about your daughter."

"She's a senior at New College. I got an e-mail from one of her professors about her absences. That's how I found out. I called the police. They looked into it, but she's an adult. They couldn't find anything—how did they put it? Nefarious. So they dropped the case."

"And her mother?"

"Deceased. When Maya was ten."

"What about boyfriends?"

"She must have had one. Or some. I don't know. She wasn't very communicative about that part of her life."

"And?"

He smiled in a very friendly way. "You're an out of work investigative reporter. I need help."

"You want to hire me to find her."

Nick nodded. "I can pay much better than any newspaper."

I glanced at my empty glass and whirled it around so the ice made that pretty tinkling sound. "How about that refill?"

CHAPTER TWO

I DROVE HOME a little drunk and confused. I hadn't taken the gig. At least not yet. I had to think about it. I poured myself a shot of tequila. The last of the good stuff I'd bought in Mexico a few years ago when I was working on a story for the paper about a migrant worker who'd been killed by Sarasota PD for no apparent reason. The paper sent me to Mexico to look for the family. I took advantage of the trip and stocked up on the best tequila I could find.

My place is an old cracker house on Hawkins Court between downtown and Sarasota Bay. I bought it back in the day when I was still married and full of illusion and the neighborhood was derelict and real estate could still be picked up by a working stiff like myself. It was a simple two-bedroom from the days when people built shit by hand. I spent three years remodeling it, which is not a big deal. With wooden houses you don't need a lot of tools and expertise. It's all carpentry. Besides, in these old places nothing's ever perfect anyway. Once you accept that, you can do anything.

I sat out on the front porch. It was a clear night. There was a gentle breeze making its way between the trees and stirring my neighbor's wind chime collection. The frogs and crickets were going at it like tiny engines humming and buzzing at intervals. My cat, Mimi, a twelve-year-old grayish tabby with a few toes missing in the front paws, came out and looked at me for maybe five seconds before she spied a lizard and dashed off to hunt.

This was one of those things I loved about living in Sarasota. My front garden was a forest of native plants: silver buttonwood, coco-plum, beach sunflower, milkweed, red penta, ferns, and a young live oak.

In the last few years the sleepy coastal Florida town I loved so much was quickly turning into a generic condo-land for the rich and famous. All the mom-and-pop restaurants had been priced out of the real estate. Now everything was expensive chichi cafés with out-door seating, snobby servers with long dark aprons and an I-don't-give-a-shit expression on their faces, five-buck espressos, and every type of chain store and restaurant you can imagine. Sarasota had lost its funkiness. But this part of downtown still had some charac-ter left. It was a whole different planet than the suburbs, than Bee Ridge or Fruitville Roads—six lanes of pavement with no trees.

I was thinking of Zavala's job offer. I wasn't sure what to make of the deal. Nick had not put out any numbers. He had been con-veniently vague about that. Not that I blamed him for it. Who the fuck was I to take this on?

I had been working on a couple of assignments for *Sarasota City Magazine*, our town's glossy lifestyle of the rich and famous publi-cation. One was a feature on a mansion that had been redecorated by one of our local celebrity designers; the other was about a couple from up north who'd bought into a new condo development on Siesta Key. Both were pure fluff—local masturbation jobs. I hated that kind of work, but it paid. The two gigs would net me about a grand. My deadline was coming up, and I hadn't even begun to write.

I went inside and poured myself another tequila. I put *The Trinity Sessions* by the Cowboy Junkies on the stereo—slow, haunting. Margo Timmins' vocals were like a massage to the brain. I needed that. I'd had one tough month after another and I was beginning to scrape the bottom of the barrel. The house was a mess, cluttered with thrift store furniture, art from local artists who never made it big, stacks of papers, books, and empty bottles of booze from my latest binge. If my life were a movie, it might look hip. But the truth was sad. This wasn't a home. My life was pathetic. My wife was gone, and I only got to see my daughter during the summers. And all the time in between we barely communicated. But what killed me was that I didn't know how to change that. I didn't know how to enjoy what little time I had with her.

On top of everything I was a few weeks away from having to cash into what little was left of my retirement. I'd have to budget, stop drinking. I had my vintage Scott stereo and a sizable vinyl collection: a lifetime of records, first press albums and special audiophile editions. I could sell it all and survive another month or two. Then what?

I knew one thing for sure: I was not going to look for another newspaper job. I'd been kicked out of the club. I had skills, a reputation, a closet full of awards. What did it get me?

I had to face it. At thirty-nine I was too old and had too much experience in a career that no longer existed. Blogs and gossip journalism had taken over the world. The prospect of working for another paper made me sick to my stomach. And really, my skills as an investigator, writer, reporter, as a person who actually gave a shit about making the world a better place, were useless. Nobody cared.

* * *

The following day I gave Nick a ring and met him at his place midafternoon. He came to the door wearing a Speedo and an unbuttoned short-sleeved shirt and dark Ray-Bans. His brown skin had that glow from sunscreen and sweat, which seems to be like a uniform for rich Floridians. Buried in his hairy chest was a gold medallion. It had the image of a man on a horse slaying a dragon, surrounded by little red gems. On the bottom corner a part of the medal was missing.

He noticed me staring at his chest and held up the medallion for me to see. "It's St. George. From Italy."

"Looks like someone took a bite out of it."

He laughed. "My grandfather was in the first war. A bullet hit him in the chest and took a part of the medallion. It saved his life."

When we walked inside, I noticed a young lady lying on a recliner by the pool. She was skinny, topless with small breasts.

"Tiffany," Nick said when he saw me checking her out. She turned on her stomach to get the sun on her back. She looked young, like a teenager. But the way she moved her body told me she knew she had something and knew how to use it.

"She's the daughter of one of the neighbors," Nick said and led me away from the window. "They like to use the pool. I don't mind."

"I wouldn't either," I said. With the tall hibiscus hedge and the wall around the garden, the place offered excellent privacy for nude sunbathing.

"A drink?" He was already at the bar.

"I think I'll wait till five."

"You know what they say. It's five o'clock somewhere."

He poured himself a bourbon. I followed him into his study. It wasn't a big room, a little dark and predictable except the shelves were stocked with sexual paraphernalia—sex toys, dildos, leather straps, chains, and all kinds of freaky sexual shit. On the side of his large oak desk was a huge erect penis.

"Louise Bourgeois," he said when he saw me staring at it. "It's an original sculpture. She made it especially for me."

"Why?"

"It's bronze," he said. "Pick it up."

"I'm fine."

He laughed. "Are you afraid of art or afraid of a penis?"

It was as long as a baseball bat with a pair of rough-looking, grapefruit-size testicles at the base. I grabbed the thing and picked it up off the desk and felt its weight. "It feels lethal."

He laughed and offered me one of the chairs. He sat across the desk. "It's how I made my fortune," he said, motioning to the sex toys. "I started out with a small sex shop in Boston's combat zone back in the early seventies. It was okay. One day one of my customers made a joke, how he had to drive all the way to downtown Boston from the suburbs just to buy a cock ring." He tapped the side of his head and grinned. "I paid attention to what he said. Six months later I took out a loan and opened a shop in Woburn. You wouldn't believe the business. Twice what I was getting downtown."

"I guess all the pervs are in the suburbs."

"No, no." He frowned. "Not perverts. That's what everybody thinks. They're just regular people. Everyone loves sex. That's what I figured out. Five years after I opened the Woburn shop, I had three more stores in Newton, Quincy, and Reading."

"Sex sells."

He laughed. "You're telling me, my friend. You're telling me."

He reached to a shelf behind him and offered me a framed photograph of an attractive young lady in a formal gown. She was elegant. Great posture. Strong dark eyes. "That's Maya," he said. "It was taken three years ago during her first year of college. I think she was going to a dance."

"She's very pretty."

"Like her mother."

I put the photograph aside. "What do you think happened?"

He shrugged. "I really have no idea. She's an A student. Brilliant. She's majoring in biology and she's already been accepted at UC Davis for graduate school."

"Did she live here?"

"No. She lived in a house near the college with roommates. She wanted the full college experience." He opened a drawer, pulled out a pad and an agenda, and wrote down an address. "Perhaps it's a place to start," he said.

I looked at the address, folded the paper, and put it in my breast pocket. "You guys didn't have a fight or anything?"

"No." Then he smiled in a way that made me think of people in jail. You ask them how they are or how it is for them and they give you this sad smile—desperate—like it's fine but it's not fine. It never will be.

"We didn't see much of each other," he said. "She had her life, I had mine. She usually came to dinner once a week. We got along but we didn't have much in common." He looked at the shelves where the sex toys were displayed. "I don't think she approved of how I made my money."

"And you say the cops found nothing suspicious?"

"Nothing."

"Do you remember the officer in charge of the investigation?"

"No," he said and looked down at his hands resting on the desk. "First it was a big man in uniform. Then it was a plainclothes detective. Then a woman in uniform." He waved his hands. "Never the same person."

I glanced at Maya's picture and leaned forward, resting my forearms on the desk. "Let me ask you something. Why don't you just hire a private investigator?"

"I tried." He showed me three pink stubby fingers. "I spoke to three. But none of them would take a missing persons case."

"You're kidding me."

"They said the same thing the cops said: 'She's an adult.' I said, 'so find her anyway,' and they said, 'no thank you.'"

I leaned back on my chair and sighed. "Maybe I shouldn't do this."

Nick's little eyes almost popped out of his face, then narrowed to a squint. "Please," he said, and reached into the drawer of his desk and pulled out a white envelope. He tossed it on the desk in front of me. "A thousand dollars a week. Plus expenses."

"Nick—"

"There's ten thousand in that envelope. It's all yours. If it takes longer, I'll give you another ten. If it takes less, you keep it all. A bonus."

All the journalism in the world had never prepared me for this type of negotiation. But it wasn't as if I wanted more. Me in my faded khakis and thrift store Hawaiian shirt, two-day stubble, and a tooth in dire need of a root canal.

I had no idea what private investigators charged for this kind of work. I just knew this was a nice chunk of change for an unemployed journalist.

"What if I can't find her?"

"You will. I know you will." His face changed again. Suddenly, he was that friendly little old man, the guy I met the previous night at Memories. He frowned, the confidence and power seeping out of him. "You have to. Please."

I'm an honest guy. Perhaps too damn honest. I couldn't see how finding someone would take more than a few days. But I wasn't a fool, either. I was broke. I needed the money. But it was more than that. Give me a mystery, a clue, an idea. That was all it took. Suddenly, I had this burning inside asking me to solve this thing, find out where this girl went. What was she doing? It was what drove me to journalism in the first place—that insatiable need to solve the puzzle.

I put the envelope in my pocket and leaned over the desk. "When was the last time you saw her?"

CHAPTER THREE

I LEFT NICK'S house and drove straight to that coffee shop on the North Trail next to New College. Before I started knocking on doors, asking about a beautiful young woman named Maya, I wanted to find out about my employer: Nick Zavala.

I ordered a double espresso, loaded it with sugar, and opened my laptop. Google had a few thousand answers for me. From what I read, Nick was being straight with me. He'd owned a string of sex shops all over New England, not just Boston. He sold out after 9/11 and moved to Florida, first Naples, then Sarasota. He also held a couple of patents on dildos he'd invented. The man had to be loaded. His house on the bay and the Lexus was nothing for someone like him. He had been married twice, divorced twice. One of his ex-wives had died of breast cancer ten years ago, about the time he'd bought the house in Sarasota, according to the County Property Assessors website.

I found nothing on the first wife and nothing on any children. Nothing about Maya Zavala or anyone else connected to him. That was a little strange, but it wasn't unusual. I Googled Maya. Nothing. Not a singe entry except her Facebook page, which was closed to those outside her circle of friends. No images, no papers, no records. Nothing from New College, nothing in the local paper or any other paper, no web or blog mentioned her name. Nothing.

I drank my coffee and got back in my car. I checked the money in the envelope. It was scary. I had never seen so many clean hundreds in my life. I didn't count them but it sure as hell looked like ten grand. I shoved the envelope under my seat and drove to the address Nick had given me.

The house was across the Trail on the corner of Old Bradenton Road and 47th, a couple of blocks from the greyhound racetrack. It was an old wooden house with a lot of windows, looked handmade. Everything in the neighborhood was old and neglected. Probably the only part of town the housing boom skipped over.

There were three cars in the driveway, an '89 Toyota Corolla, a Nissan pickup, and a '70s Mercedes diesel with flat tires and the windows open. There were three bicycles on the ground by the front door. All the plants in the yard were overgrown. Kudzu was overtaking the oak tree and the side fence. A black cat slept by the recycling bins that were full of empty beer cans.

I knocked on the door. There was music. Sounded like the Grateful Dead. I knocked again. Nothing. I pushed the door open real slow.

I called out, "Hello?"

Bits of conversation and laughter came over the music.

"Hello?" The place stank of cigarette smoke, pot, incense, and dirty socks. It was a mess. Three young men and two young women were sprawled on a set of couches in the living room. They looked as if they'd just been pulled out of Haight-Ashbury circa 1968.

"Hey, man, just come on in." The guy with the long red hair and wiry glasses sat up. He looked just like a male version of Janis Joplin. The others stopped talking. One of the women, the small one with the paisley headband, turned the volume down on the stereo.

"Who're you, man?" one of the other guys said. He was chunky with curly hair—Jerry Garcia.

"I'm a friend of Maya's," I said.

They fell silent. The girl with the paisley headband looked at Janis Joplin and back at me. "You're a cop," she said. "Don't you have to identify yourself or something?"

"You got a warrant?" Janis Joplin said.

"I'm not a cop. I'm a friend of her family's."

They stared at each other, at me, their red glassy eyes focusing back and forth like they didn't know where to park themselves.

"You look like a cop," Jerry Garcia said.

"You smell like a cop," Janis Joplin said. That threw them into a laughing fit.

I took a deep breath.

"We don't know shit," Paisley said.

"She lives here. You mind telling me about it?"

"Dude," Janis Joplin said. "We don't know shit. That's what she just said. She lived here for like five months. She kept to herself. And then she split. Fucked us up on the rent."

"A real drag," Jerry Garcia said.

"Where did she split to?"

Jerry Garcia shook his head. "We don't want any hassles, man."

"Look," I said. "I'm not a cop. I'm a reporter and a friend of the family. They asked me to help them find her. They're worried. I mean, what if it was your daughter who vanished?"

"No way, man." Paisley laughed. "Like, we don't reproduce."

"I'm just saying. If you did."

"But we don't."

"Did she leave anything behind?"

They looked at each other. I thought of two things: they were hiding something or they were just stoned and didn't give a shit. Most likely it was the latter. I moved closer and sat on the corner of the couch. The ashtray was full of roaches and cigarette butts. There was a plastic bong on the carpet. The place was filthy. I couldn't imagine Maya, the elegant young woman from the picture, living in a place like this.

"You seen her at school lately?" I asked.

Janis Joplin flinched, looked at Jerry Garcia.

I pulled out my phone. "Look, I could call the cops, tell them about all the dope you have lying around this place."

"Ah, come on," Paisley said. "Uncool."

"Tell me about Maya?"

"She had Hannah's room," Janice Joplin said and glanced at Jerry Garcia. "She was here for like what, four or five months?"

"Then what happened?"

Janice Joplin shook his head. "Dude, she just split. People come and go from this house all the time."

"Can't keep track, man," Jerry Garcia added.

"And you don't know where she went," I said.

Janis Joplin grinned. "I'm not her father, man."

"Where's Hannah?"

They looked at each other. Jerry Garcia shrugged. "She's at school."

A hippy flophouse. Who knew who held the lease, maybe Janis. Maybe no one. People came and went, paid and stayed, no strings attached.

It was obvious I wasn't going to get anywhere with these clowns. I walked out. A girl in a loose cotton skirt and a tie-dye t-shirt was just getting off her bike in front of the house.

"Are you Hannah?"

She smiled. "That's me."

"I was looking for Maya. The guys in the house said you might know where she is?"

"Who're you?"

"I'm with the UC Davis graduate school. Microbiology."

She looked me up and down. "For real?"

I nodded. "We haven't heard from her since we accepted her into the program."

Hannah chuckled, curled a strand of hair behind her ear. "You must really want her."

"We certainly do."

She tilted her head to the side and bit her fingernail.

"So how long did she live here, anyway?"

She raised her eyes. "She never really lived here."

"Really?"

"She just used it as an address. She came and got her mail every week and gave Kirk a check every month."

"Who's Kirk?"

"The guy with the red hair." The Janis Joplin character.

"So what happened?"

She shrugged. "She just stopped coming by, I guess. I mean, I don't really know her."

"When was this?"

"I don't know. Like a month ago. Or two. I didn't pay any attention."

"Do you know where she lives now?"

She dropped her head and looked away. "She has a boyfriend."

"Oh." I laughed. "They moved in together."

She nodded.

"Do you know his name?"

"Mike."

"Does he go to New College?"

She shook her head. "He's older. He works, I guess."

"What's Mike's last name?"

"Mike . . . Baseman or Bossman or Boseman or something like that. It started with a B and ended with man. Something like that."

"So she paid rent here but lived with this guy."

"I guess she didn't want her parents to know she was living with him."

"So you know where Mike lives?"

"I think Siesta."

"Seriously?"

She nodded and glanced past me at the house.

"Do you know where on Siesta?" Siesta Key was Sarasota's beach paradise—every year it was voted best beach in the universe by some magazine or another.

She shook her head. "No, but I heard Maya say it was a great place. She said it was like the *real Florida*. Whatever that means."

CHAPTER FOUR

By the time I left the hippy house it was late afternoon. I went straight to happy hour at Caragiulos on Palm Avenue in downtown. I was starving. And I wanted to celebrate my progress and plan my next move. Caragiulos had been in Sarasota long before all the chichi places moved in. It wasn't one hundred percent my thing, but the narrow bar with the brick wall and the nice spread they set out for happy hour always hit the spot.

I took a seat at the far end of the bar—way in the back. I had decided to approach finding Maya the way I approached working on a story: notes. I opened a new document in my laptop, titled it *Maya*, and put it all down—everything about Nick, everything about the hippies, my theories. Everything I saw and heard. I put it all down.

I had some fried calamari, a pressed panini, a few cold Birra Moretti. Pretty soon I found myself in a decent little groove. My brain was churning like a steamroller. I made a few searches for Maya. Then I tried variations on Mike Boseman.

Google gave me the skinny on Boseman pretty damn quick. He was all over the web. His fifteen minutes of fame came a few years ago when he promised to bring Hollywood to Sarasota. He suckered the city and county governments to dish big bucks for his movie venture. You'd think he was Steven Spielberg.

Boseman had made a small fortune when he invented a gizmo that helped advance rearview cameras in cars. He sold the patent and came to Sarasota to open a big movie studio. He made all kinds of promises: everyone in California would follow him to our pretty little town if Sarasota was willing to lend a hand. Our starstruck city council was giddy with the prospect of Hollywood celebrities hanging in our outdoor cafés. They threw money at him, two million to be exact. He was going to open a soundstage and bring people in *the biz* to town and start filming right away. But no one bothered to check his record. The man knew nobody in Hollywood. The closest he'd ever been to a movie was Netflix. He was just another greedy businessman with the gift of gab. He had no company and no title. The *Sarasota Herald* did a number of stories on him—all of them shiny profiles saying how he was going to put our little slice of paradise on the map. He managed to produce a pilot that never sold. Then the company closed shop. At the center of the fiasco was Mr. Michael Boseman.

The city sued him. He counter-sued. And guess what? He won. Motherfucker got a million-dollar claim and got into real estate. Pumped all his money into condos. When the mortgage crisis hit, it all came tumbling down.

I didn't even know he was still in town. I'd imagine he'd run for the border, left the country, disappeared just like Maya Zavala. But here he was living the life on Siesta Key. I couldn't wait to find out what his game was.

I was pretty drunk and was just getting ready to stumble home, when I noticed Holly Lovett sitting at a table near the front of the bar with a couple of friends.

Holly Holly Holly. Of all the gin joints... Holly was pretty without being beautiful, smart without being pompous, liberal without being overbearing. And she was a lawyer without being an asshole.

I hadn't seen her in three years.

I'd met Holly when she worked with an advocacy group for migrant workers in downtown Bradenton, north of Sarasota. I was working on that story about the Mexican migrant who'd been shot by Sarasota PD. We hit it off right away. We were perfect together. We were almost identical: ambitious, driven, idealistic. We laughed and argued politics and had great sex without too much attachment. The energy between us was tremendous. Then I went to Mexico to find the family of the victim. I was gone for three weeks. Three fucking weeks. When I came back, she had hooked up with this douchebag accident lawyer. Joaquin del Pino. His commercials were all over TV. "Joaquin del Pino, Justice for All. Se habla Español." Total ass.

Now she was sitting half a dozen stools from me and looking as beautiful as ever. She wore a tight business suit; her blond hair was combed back in a perfect bun. And like always, her pretty lips were painted bright red. She looked great. She always did.

I can be tough in an interview. I can help out some old guy who's getting the crap beat out of him. I can travel to strange lands where I don't speak the language. I can look a cop in the face and accuse him of lying to a grand jury. But I couldn't face Holly. Not now. I was a laid-off, has-been reporter. My self-esteem was in the gutter. And I was drunk.

I felt like I was back in middle school. I wanted out of the bar. I wanted to go home and sleep it off. I didn't want Holly to see me like this—drunk and down and miserable.

But to leave the bar I had to squeeze right past her. It was the only way out. I closed my laptop, paid my bill, and stood. On the one hand, I was hoping she wouldn't notice me, but on the other, I was hoping she would, that she'd say she'd dropped her Justice for All attorney, that she missed me, that we should get together sometime. Maybe that she wanted to come home with me.

I shoved my laptop in my bag and focused on the exit—walked the walk.

"Dexter?" Her voice hadn't changed. It still had that magic timbre like the song of a siren. She turned her body and leaned back on her chair as I passed. "Is that you?"

"Holly," I said full of fake surprise. "Long time no see."

She grabbed my arm and pulled me toward her and gave me a hug. She still smelled like heaven. Then she kissed me on the cheek and squeezed my arm like she was more than a friend.

"What have you been up to?" Before I could answer, she introduced me to her friends—two women lawyers. They were out celebrating because one of them had just opened her own practice. I registered none of that, but I latched on to Holly's pretty green eyes and the red smile that reminded me of sitting with her on the porch of my house, holding hands, and talking of how the two us were going to turn this shitty tourist trap of a town into a place where everyone could live a decent life.

"Grab a chair," she said and wiped the lipstick mark from my cheek with her thumb. "Please join us."

I pulled a stool and sat as close to her as I could—my leg touching hers, my arm around the back of her stool. I wanted to breathe her in, take in the smell I'd been missing for three years. I set my bag down by my feet and ordered a tequila. The best shit they had was Don Julio. Good enough. At this point even Cuervo would have worked for me.

"I've missed you," she said and held my hand like we were lovers. "After I read about the layoffs, I was afraid you'd moved out of town."

I shook my head. "They can't run me out of paradise."

"Did you find another job?"

"Kind of." I didn't want to tell her what I was up to. Not because I was embarrassed, but because I didn't know. Or maybe I was embarrassed. She was Holly Lovett for fuck's sake. I wanted to present a perfect picture. I wanted another chance with her. "I'm working on a couple of freelance pieces. I have a few irons in the fire."

She rubbed my back. "I'm so glad to hear that, babe."

Babe? Really?

"What's new with you?" I said trying to sound as casual and as sober as I could. "Last I heard you were engaged or something."

She laughed, but it was obviously forced.

"Joaquin and I broke up," she said. "I guess we were just not meant to be."

"That's too bad." I could hardly contain my glee.

"It wasn't easy," she said. "But it's all in the past now."

"We should get together." It came out of me like a pro, full of confidence. Bravado. "Let me take you out to dinner."

"That would be nice, Dex."

I smiled. I had her. My day—my night—couldn't have gotten any better. But I was drunk and I had all that Maya Zavala shit reeling in my mind.

"I have to go," I said. "I have some work I have to finish up."

"Sure, babe."

"I'll call you tomorrow," I said. "We'll go to Michael's on East. Remember?"

She smiled big—teeth, squinty eyes, the works. "My God, you remember. We always talked about going there." She stood and took my face in her soft hands and kissed me full on the lips with just the slightest hint of tongue.

I walked out while I still could. I left my car where it was parked and walked, my legs wobbling all the way home.

It was hard to believe. In three years I had never bumped into her in this little town. And now there she was. And she had broken up with the Justice for All lawyer. I couldn't wait to hear how it had gone down.

But I had to focus. I had to think of Maya and Boseman. I had to look him up. Find Boseman, find Maya. By all accounts Boseman was a sleaze. What if he did something to her?

No. I was getting ahead of myself. I had to erase the prejudice, clear the slate. I knew nothing. What Boseman had done before had no relation to Maya. No matter how I felt about him, this wasn't about busting Boseman. This was about finding Maya.

CHAPTER FIVE

IT WAS ALMOST ten when I awoke the following morning. My AC had conked out. It was eighty-eight degrees in the house and I was soaked in sweat. I had a headache and was dizzy from the booze. Mimi, that mischievous and lucky cat, was lying on the pillow next to my bed. Good morning to you.

I shuffled to the bathroom, drank water, washed my face. Last night was a fog. I retraced my steps. I had been in Caragiulos, gotten drunk, and left my car parked on Palm Avenue. I had seen Holly. Or was that an illusion, a dream? She kept calling me *babe*. And she kissed me.

Maya Zavala. Right. I was right on her trail. Today I had to find Boseman. I searched around my messy house. My laptop was gone.

The restaurant. I'd also left an envelope with ten grand under the seat of my car.

Fuck. Me.

I didn't shower. I just fed Mimi a handful of dry food and ran back to Caragiulos. My car was still there, intact—a twenty-five-dollar parking ticket on the windshield. Caragiulos was just opening for lunch. I asked the manager about my bag, a small leather case with a laptop. He seemed skeptical. He went back to ask the kitchen staff. I had everything in there. All the information, the stupid stories I was working on for the magazine, my leads for finding Maya, the info on Boseman.

After about twenty minutes the manager came back. He had the bag. Yes. He had the bag. He handed it over with a smile that seemed to say: you lucky bastard. It was all in there, computer, notebooks, pens, gum.

Before driving out to Boseman's place on Siesta Key, I drove by the bank and deposited half of the ten grand into my checking account. Then I went home and stashed the other five in the pages of Diana Kennedy's *Recipes from the Regional Cooks of Mexico.* The house was so hot, it stank of old wood and that unique sour smell of termite shit. I called the AC repairman. They said the earliest they could send someone was at the end of the day.

* * *

Siesta Key is the little island that made me fall in love with Sarasota back in '95 when I came down with a couple of buddies from the University of Houston for spring break. I knew I would come back. But in my overactive imagination I always thought I'd own a place on the beach. It didn't seem so far-fetched back then. Real estate seemed affordable, and I had the crazy illusion that I'd become a well-paid, hotshot journalist. So much for that pipe dream.

I had gotten Boseman's address from the County Assessors website. It was a large house by Point of Rocks at the very south end of the public beach, the one I never went to anymore because trekking out there, finding parking, and dealing with the crowds took all the fun out of it. I liked nature, quiet. Siesta Beach lost that long ago.

I drove past the village and the beach and turned into Point of Rocks Road and found the house. It was pretty much like all the other houses on the Gulf, but it wasn't as obnoxious as I had imagined it would be. It was an older two-story place with a lot of wood and character. It was the kind of place I could live in if I were rich. I knocked on the door but got no answer. I stepped back and looked at the small windows. Nothing. No movement, no lights. A late-model silver Jaguar XJ was parked in front of the garage. I walked back to the front door and knocked again.

I went back to my car. It was early afternoon. Maybe he had a job or had gone out to lunch, which wasn't such a bad idea. I drove to Anna's Deli a few blocks away and devoured a Pastrami Ruben with extra sauerkraut and Tabasco. It cured my hangover like a magic potion.

About an hour later I went back to Boseman's place. The Jaguar was still there. I knocked, got nothing. I walked to the side and down to the beach access path. Then I made my way toward his house from the beach side. The erosion had washed out most of the sand so anyone walking the beach had to walk across the backyards of the houses.

I climbed past the private property sign. The rear of the house was all windows. I imagined every room had a view of the ocean. The patio was all stone around a small kidney-shaped pool. A hammock hung between two palm trees. On a table by the pool there was a pair of women's sunglasses, red and big like butterfly wings. I picked them up. Vintage Dior from the '50s. There were two empty glasses, one with lipstick marks, a tube of Hawaiian Tropic, and a Victoria's Secret catalogue.

I made my way around the pool to the sliding glass door and knocked. I started to think maybe Mike Boseman had absconded with Maya Zavala. Maybe they'd eloped. Maybe Nick really had nothing to worry about. I understood that he wanted to know his daughter was all right, but really, if she chose to take a six-month trip to Luxembourg with Boseman or some other hack, that was her choice. She didn't have to notify him or anyone else if she didn't want to.

When I turned to go, someone yelled, "Hey, get the fuck off my property!"

I put my hand over my brow to shield my eyes from the sun and get a better look. It was him. Mike Boseman in the flesh. I recognized him right away from the photos I'd seen on the computer and from the newspaper article where he was posing with his production manager—a tall sexy blond—and a fancy Bell helicopter parked in front of the new sound studio warehouse of his now defunct Sarasota film production company.

He was leaning out a window on the second floor, shirtless, his shoulder-length hair a mess. He looked like a surfer—a wealthy beach bum.

"I got a sign posted, asshole. You blind?"

"Yeah, I saw it." I took a couple of steps back so I didn't have to crane my neck so steep. "But no one was answering the front door. I'd like to have a word with you, Mr. Boseman."

It took him a moment, like he was surprised that I called him by his last name. He stared at me, probably sizing me up. "What's this about?"

"If you don't mind, I'd rather not be yelling it out for all your neighbors to hear."

Again he just stared. He didn't look pleased. He glanced back into the room and then back at me.

"I'm not selling anything and I'm not with the government," I said.

"You with the paper?"

"Not anymore."

"Do I know you?"

"My name's Dexter Vega. I want to talk to you about a mutual friend."

"Oh, yeah?"

I spread my arms. It was hot. The sun was burning overhead. I needed a drink. "Five minutes."

Again, he took a moment. He looked back inside. Maybe there was someone there with him. Then he closed the window. A minute later he opened the sliding glass door and walked out on the patio to meet me. He was wearing khaki cargo shorts and nothing else. His skin was red and brown and slightly peeling on his nose and shoulders from the sun. He must have been spending a lot of time out on the beach.

He crossed his arms over his bare chest. "Five minutes."

"I'm trying to find Maya Zavala."

There was a subtle twinge in his blue eyes. "What makes you think I know where she is?" he asked.

"You're her boyfriend. She lived with you. I figured you might know something."

He leaned back and raised his head. He was tall, strong. He looked to be my age, but fit. I could tell he was sharp. I suppose you had to be to bamboozle the county out of three million bucks and stay out of jail all in a single bound.

"Where did you hear that?" he said.

He was asking a lot of questions, a clear sign of guilt. I was on to something with him, but I needed to coax it out of him. Gently. "We've got mutual friends. They're worried about her."

"What mutual friends? Give me some names."

I took a shot in the dark: "John and Mary."

"You mean Joey and May."

"No," I said. "John and Mary, from New College."

He squinted. "What's your game, man?"

"I told you. I'm looking for Maya. It's like she suddenly dropped off the face of the earth. Her friends are worried."

"Maya doesn't have any friends."

So he did know her. "Where is she?"

For the first time he smiled. "What makes you think I know?"

"I'm not a cop, and I'm not planning on going to the cops. But I could. I could also go to the paper. Can you see it? Pretty co-ed disappears, former Sarasota-Hollywood exec is prime suspect."

"Why do you want her?" he asked.

I was getting warm. He sounded worried, or maybe not. I changed my tone, gentle but firm. "Her biology professor at New College came to me. We're old friends. He told me he was worried about her, asked me to look into it. That's it."

"Dr. Tabor?"

I nodded. "We just want to know she's okay."

"She's fine."

"Where is she?"

"I thought Dr. Tabor knew she was going."

"He did," I said. "But he lost touch. He hasn't heard from her in a while."

"Maybe he's getting old. The whole fieldwork idea was his suggestion."

"Fieldwork?"

"To count those damn Mexican salamanders. The axo-whatever the fuck they're called."

I nodded. "So she's in Mexico."

"Yeah, it's all over her Facebook page."

I stepped back. "I don't do Facebook."

"Dr. Tabor does. He knows everything about the trip. He set the whole thing up."

"Shit. Maybe he is getting old."

He shook his head. "I'm telling you. He knows more about what she's up to than I do."

"Damn that Dr. Tabor. He made me come down here for nothing."

Boseman laughed. "Hey, I'm sorry about earlier. I get all kinds of assholes walking across my property to get to the other side of the beach."

"No sweat. I'd get pissed if I had someone hanging out in my backyard."

* * *

I left Siesta Key and headed north toward New College. Dr. Tabor. That was the lead. I'd thought about going to him earlier, but I didn't imagine a college professor would know much about the personal life of one of his students.

On the way I called Holly and left her a voice mail about getting together. I'd invited her to Michael's on East, a nice fancy restaurant—old school and classy. I reextended the invitation, suggested tonight or tomorrow. Whatever worked best for her. Last night was still sketchy in my brain. I was dying to find out if what I remembered really happened the way I thought it did. I didn't want to get my hopes up for nothing. With Holly you never knew. And with Holly, I was playing with fire. I didn't want to get burned again.

* * *

I've never been one to face authority straight on. As a matter of fact, I had a serious disdain for people in positions of power, people who needed to have control and buried themselves in their own bureaucracy. Still, when I arrived at New College, I went straight to the administration building and asked for Dr. Tabor.

Big mistake. Right away they needed to see my ID. They unloaded a barrage of questions: Who was I, why did I want to see him, did I have an appointment, could I fill out this form?

After about twenty minutes of bullshit, I just walked out. I drove across the campus and pulled over by a group of students and asked them where I might find Tabor. They pointed me to the biology labs.

Tabor was in his office. He was a short man with wire-rim glasses and a twitch in his left eye. He was in his late fifties, overweight, and pink in the face from either too much booze or too much sun. His office was tiny, like a large cubicle. And extremely well organized. It kind of made him look larger than he was. On the back wall he had a few framed diplomas and awards—a shrine to his academic ego.

"Of course, I know Maya," he said when I asked about her. "But I can't discuss a student unless you're a family member, or unless Maya has cleared you to receive information about her academic standing—"

"I'm not here for anything like that. I just want to know where she is."

"What makes you think I know?" He sat up, straightened his back, and squinted, his left eyelid trembling.

"Apparently she's gone to Mexico to study a salamander or something," I said. "Not that there's anything wrong with that. But her family has lost contact with her and they're worried sick."

"And you're family?"

"Kind of," I said. "I'm a good friend. They asked me to look into her whereabouts. They're afraid maybe she was kidnapped. Mexico's not the safest place to hang out."

"Well." He sounded flustered. "They need to contact the administration. You can't just come in here asking—"

I leaned over his desk. "Look, Doc. Take it easy. We don't have to make a big deal about this, okay? I just want to find out where she is."

He pushed his glasses up on his nose. Then he reached for his computer mouse and made a few clicks.

I leaned against the wall and crossed my arms. "I'm not trying to be threatening, but you were the one who encouraged her to go to Mexico. If anything happened to her . . ."

He raised his eyes at me. "Who told you that?"

"Everyone knows. It's on the record."

"Are you with the police?"

"Why would you ask that?"

"If you are, you need to identify yourself as a law enforcement officer. There are protocols."

I leaned forward, placed my hands on his desk, looked him in the eyes. "Spill it, Tabor."

"What are you talking about? I have nothing to hide." He stood and hung his hands on the sides of his waist. "I suggest you leave. I'll call security."

"No problem," I said and dropped down on the only other chair in the room. "Call whoever you want. I can't wait to let them know what happened to Maya and how you incited her to travel alone to a place that the U.S. Department of State has issued warnings about. You put her in danger."

He stared at me, then past me, past the door at the hallway. "What's your problem?"

"I told you. I want to know where she is. I want an address."

"But I don't know—"

"Facebook, Doctor. Log in and get me her info. Now."

He shuddered and sat back down. The keys on his computer began to sing. In a moment he started reciting her info. "She's in Mexico City, but there's no address, just Colonia Roma and that she's working with a team from the university in Xochimilco."

I came around the desk and glanced at the Facebook page on the screen. Her profile picture was a funny-looking salamander with little arms and beady purple eyes. Her last post was two weeks ago. She'd been searching for the little critter near the Island of Dolls.

"Has she sent you any e-mails?"

He shook his head. "She sent me a couple of e-mails when she first arrived to let me know she had arranged for a tour of Xochimilco with the Biology department from the university—"

"What university?"

"UNAM, National Autonomous University of Mexico."

"Did she mention any friends, colleagues, roommates?"

Tabor pushed his chair back and moved away from the computer, gave me a sly smile. "Maya Zavala has no friends."

I couldn't imagine a pretty, elegant young woman like Maya not having friends, an entourage, even. "Four years in college and not a single friend?"

Tabor shrugged. "You know Maya."

"Not really," I said. "Tell me."

"She's quiet. And very ambitious. She works harder than any student who's ever come through my department."

"Still," I said. "She could have had a friend. At least a lab partner or something."

"Not Maya." He gave me a sly smile. "Perhaps it's a character flaw."

Her boyfriend was rich. Her father was a millionaire. I suppose she could be abrasive. Maybe she was an asshole. You can't tell someone's personality from a photograph. "Tell me about these critters, the salamanders."

"I didn't put her up to it. I just mentioned the—"

"There's no need to get defensive, Doc. Just tell me about them. That's why she went, right?"

He took a deep breath. "The axolotl is a fascinating animal. They're amphibious but never grow lungs. And they can regenerate limbs. But they've disappeared from the wild. Maya knew about them. We study them in class. Well, not real axolotl, but we look at various animals with peculiar anomalies and how their mutations and genes are affected by environment. Like sharks. We look at how their—"

"You're getting on a tangent."

He stopped and fixed his glasses. "Right. Well, I mentioned, perhaps in passing, how . . . if someone found an axolotl in the wild it would be quite an achievement. Something like that could make someone's career."

"You didn't think she would jump on the next plane to Mexico."

"Of course not. It's not as if I told her a big secret. I was addressing the class. We were talking about research they might take on, projects that could help them get into graduate school or find publication for their papers in academic journals. One of my students made a smart comment about how all the great subjects had been tackled. I was only trying to make a point."

"Right. And so if Maya or anyone else found one of these critters, they'd get published. Instant fame."

"It's a big deal. These animals are endemic to Mexico City. The valley where the city is built was a series of lakes during the time of the Aztecs. The axolotl hasn't changed in thousands of years. They're fascinating—"

"Except they don't really exist anymore."

He shook his head. "Not in the wild."

I left it at that. I was beginning to get a pretty good picture of Maya Zavala. What I didn't get was why she wasn't communicating with Boseman or her father or Dr. Tabor. Ambitious or not, you'd think she'd at least send a postcard, let someone know she was okay.

And then there was her Facebook page. She might not have friends in Sarasota, but she had over two hundred friends on Facebook. But that didn't mean much. They could have been colleagues, contacts. Who knew?

I wanted to swing by Nick's place on my way home and give him the news, but I was running late to meet the AC repairman at my house. I sure as hell wasn't going to spend another night in that sweat lodge. And then there was Holly. She hadn't called back. It had my gut in a knot. If I had another chance to fix things with her, I was going to go all out. What I needed now was a drink for courage.

CHAPTER SIX

THE AC REPAIRMAN arrived. He had to change a $120 gizmo in my air handler. At least Mimi didn't seem to mind the heat. She was lying in my desk chair like she owned the damn thing.

I pulled a cold beer from the fridge and called Holly again. It went right to voice mail. I began to grow paranoid. Maybe the whole thing had been hatched up in my drunken imagination. Maybe the reason I was so taken with her had to do with the fact that we never really completed our relationship. We'd had no real definition. We were never really an item, but it was more than just dating. It was a strange, noncommittal relationship. We were best friends. We had sex—great, fun sex. And then it was over. Just like that. We both let it go. But deep down I'd wanted more. I'd wanted to make a go of it—try for the real thing. But you know what they say: if you love someone, set them free. So like a fool, I let her go. Only then did I realize she was never mine to begin with.

But like my good friend the photographer Rachel Mann told me while I drowned my sorrows after losing Holly, no girl wants freedom. She said what Holly really wanted was to see me step up to the plate, tell her I loved her, offer commitment.

Of course, Rachel was gay. What did she know? And she was too late with her advice anyway. We were drinking at the Bahi Hut, an old drinking hole on the North Trail. I was in miserable shape. I had just learned that Holly had hooked up with del Pino. Rachel stroked my hair, ordered another round of Mai Tais, and gave me the most solid piece of advice on women anyone has ever given me: "You need to make a woman feel like she's wanted. Read between the lines. Fight for her. Show her you give a shit."

That was three years ago when I was a fool and totally full of my-self—when I still believed in journalism. And in myself. It took me almost forty years to learn the greatest life lesson: never put your career ahead of your own happiness.

I'm bitter. I'm bitter about drinking the fucking Kool-Aid and believing all the bullshit they fed me in journalism school. I'm bitter about my divorce, about the paper, about not seeing Zoe enough, about what happened to my father. And, yeah, I'm also bitter about my breakup with Holly.

I called Holly again. Still no answer. Maybe she was avoiding me. Paranoia began to crawl over me. No. I needed to chill. We needed to start over clean. We needed to do it right this time. One thing I was sure about was that I had to act soon. She'd dropped the lawyer. I had to make my move before another one of those vultures in suits snatched her away.

* * *

The AC repairman finished his work. The vents in the old house blowing cold shook me out of my daze. I pushed my thoughts of Holly aside and focused on what was important: Maya Zavala. Now, there was a mystery woman. She was pretty, ambitious, and obviously rich. She had everything anyone could want, and yet there she was in some muck lake in Mexico digging for reptiles like a ten-year-old boy.

I was intrigued. I couldn't figure why I couldn't find anything on the web about her. It got me going. I mean, who has a nonexistent digital footprint these days?

But there was something else. I stared at her picture for a long time. There was something in her eyes, like a wisdom beyond her years. She must have been seventeen, maybe eighteen when the photograph was taken. She looked like a senior going to the prom. But she also looked like a woman. Like someone who had lived and was already jaded by life. There was a sadness, a cynicism—something dark behind her large brown eyes.

By seven p.m. Holly still hadn't called. It was too late to make dinner plans, especially at a nice place like Michael's on East. Without a reservation, we'd never get a table. And that was the date—the place where I could swoon her to my side. That's what we'd dreamed of doing in the old days.

Nothing was going to happen—not tonight. I texted her and told her to call me tomorrow. Right now I had to deal with business. I called Nick. I had to give him the news. Maya was in old Mexico. I imagined he'd be thrilled. But as the phone rang, I felt my stomach do a little dance. What if he asked for some money back?

I had only worked two days for ten grand. Then again, he might ask me to go to Mexico.

There was no answer. I left him a vague voice mail. I figured some things should not be left on machines. I just said we needed to talk so we could move forward. When I hung up I fed Mimi, took a shower, drank the last beer in the house, and left. My plan was to stop in at Nick's, give him the lowdown, then pop over to Memories Lounge and get happy.

The sun had just set behind the bay when I turned off the North Trail and approached Nick's house. Blue and red lights reflected on the hood of my Subaru like Christmas decorations. Five police cruisers crowded the driveway. At first it was like a dream, like it couldn't be happening in the place where I was going, that Nick's place was not surrounded by cops, that my job had either ended or gotten complicated.

The officers were Sarasota PD. That was better than dealing with the hillbillies from the County sheriff's office. I pulled up on the side, just off Bay Shore, slightly ahead of the driveway, and walked back toward the house.

A handful of neighbors were standing in a tight group staring at the circus. The good citizens of Sapphire Shores dressed in shorts and t-shirts maintaining a polite distance from the action, taking photos with their smartphones, gossiping. I was sure their curiosity was burning like wildfire.

I walked up the driveway. Then I saw the crime scene van. It was like walking into a crooked photograph. The cops were moving in slow motion, talking among themselves outside the house. One of them saw me coming, and as if by some secret order, they all turned and stared, waiting for me to reach them. Then the fat one with the sergeant stripes raised his hand to stop me.

The whole gig flashed before my eyes: the ten grand, Maya Zavala, the topless girl, the damn salamanders.

"Sir," the fat cop said. He had a wide gap between his two front teeth. "No one's allowed through. One of my officers will be taking statements from the neighbors in a few minutes. If you—"

"I'm not a neighbor."

"You with the paper?" he asked.

"Yeah." I spotted Rachel Mann, her black curly hair and a pair of heavy Canon cameras hanging on her skinny little neck. She was talking to Detective Jack Petrillo at the entrance to the house. I called out: "Rachel!"

She waved. The big sergeant saw this and moved aside, letting me pass. I joined Petrillo and Rachel by the front door.

Rachel gave me an awkward hug, her cameras pressing against my stomach. "I got some serious gossip for you," I said.

"What are you doing here?"

"Isn't that what he's supposed to ask?"

Rachel smiled and laced her arm around mine. "We're a team."

Detective Petrillo grinned. "He's no longer with the paper."

"So?" I said. "I'm still a member of the press. What's going on here?"

Petrillo hesitated, but his ego was his biggest weakness. One day he was going to be chief of police, mayor of the city, governor of the Sunshine State. His ego was either going to make his career or destroy it. But right now that's what gave us leverage. We were press. He wanted the attention. He ran his hand over his thick mane of black hair, the stink of too much Paco Rabanne polluting the air. He gave us a politician's smile full of straight white teeth. "We have a body. We're treating it as a homicide."

My knees felt weak. I grabbed Rachel's arm.

"Can we go in and take a look?" she asked. She was relentless. Her livelihood depended on it. If she was working for the paper, she was either getting a hundred bucks for the assignment or fifty for a picture. No picture, no money. It was a shit life.

Petrillo seemed to be weighing the request, considering the pros and cons, probably wondering how to capitalize on the moment.

"Officer Gasanov," he called to the fat cop in the driveway. "I'm taking these folks in for a quick tour. No one comes inside."

Gasanov nodded and turned back to face the street where more neighbors had gathered. There were kids on bikes, couples with dogs. It was a real show.

When we walked into the living room, Rachel spied the Warhol. "Nice."

"Fake," Petrillo announced.

"Bullshit," I said.

"Well, probably," he corrected himself. "No one has an art collection like this unless they're a museum."

"Maybe the guy had taste," I said.

"And beaucoup bucks," Petrillo said and led us into the study—the same place where Nick had tossed me an envelope with ten grand two days ago. I averted my eyes, my brain racing with all the possible implications. My message was probably still in his voice mail. This wasn't good.

When Rachel saw all the sexual paraphernalia lining the shelves, she smiled and raised her camera. "What is this, paradise?"

Petrillo shook his head and placed his arm around Rachel. He reined her in. "No pictures, okay? Please."

"Come on, Detective. Give me a break."

"Not here," he said. "Not right now."

Rachel gave me a look. But I had my own problems.

Two women with the medical examiners office were taking notes, both of them wearing blue latex gloves, Nikon's hanging from their necks. One of them looked familiar. She had a pierced nose and dyed black hair, like Joan Jett. Rachel leaned close to me. "She's the guitar player of the Funky Donkeys."

I had seen the band once, couldn't remember the music. The woman nodded at Rachel, gave her a brief smile. I glanced at Rachel. She grinned and whispered in my ear: "I fucked her."

A plainclothes detective was crouched down behind the desk where a white sheet covered the body of Nick Zavala. A pool of blood had run down the grout lines of the tile to the edge of the Persian rug where the giant penis sculpture by Louise Bourgeois lay on the floor, a police tag taped to one of the testicles.

"Death by penis." Petrillo laughed.

It almost knocked me over.

The detective who was examining the body stood. "What the hell is this, Petrillo?" He had a light southern accent. He didn't look happy.

"It's okay." Petrillo made a gesture with his hand. "It's just for background. No photos." Then he looked at me. "Everything's off the record."

I raised my hands to show him I agreed. My hands trembled. I brought them down quick, forced a smile. I had never seen the detective before. He was young, maybe late twenties, and very pale. "So what do you think happened?"

The detective glared at me. Then he turned to Petrillo. "Chief Miller hears about this, it's your ass."

Miller was Jennifer Miller, the chief of police. Maybe that was the card Petrillo was playing. I knew Chief Miller and she knew me. I had embarrassed her after an article I wrote on how the cops in this town are a bunch of morons who have zero accountability when arresting or shooting people caused a big stink. The report led to an official investigation. It found that the department was not following procedure in at least 30 percent of arrests where excessive force had been used. The cops especially liked to beat up on homeless people and minorities. Sarasota PD promptly lost their accreditation. They were not the worst police force in the country. Not by a long shot. But they were ignorant and full of themselves.

"Take it easy, Frey," Petrillo said. He was cautious, like a man playing chess. "I'll take full responsibility."

Petrillo had been with the force eleven years. He was a pro. He knew how to play people, managed to stay alive when everyone else got chopped. Now, he sounded as if he was daring this new detective to cross him.

The detective turned his eyes to me and reluctantly spilled a handful of beans. "Someone beat his head to a pulp with that giant dildo."

Petrillo glanced at me. "No sign of a forced entry."

The detective frowned, stepped over the body, and stomped quickly out of the study.

"Don't mind Detective Frey," Petrillo said. "He's new."

"Was there a struggle?" I asked. I was thinking of the rough guy at the bar and the pounding he gave Nick.

Petrillo shook his head. "The perpetrator must have known the victim. But whoever did it went above and beyond." He looked past the medical examiners. "There's brain matter and cranium fragments all over the shelves. His head was mush. Literally."

"Another beautiful day in paradise," I said. It was an act on my part. I was freaking. That was Nick under that sheet. And I'd just been dealing with him. A tense and shitty mix of guilt and fear pushed up my throat. I felt like throwing up.

My eyes moved all over the study, trying to record everything: the dildos on the shelf—now splattered with dark blood stains— the papers on the desk, the computer monitor, the pens in a penholder, the Andres Serrano sketch of multiple tiny penises hanging on a side wall, the photographs of Nick as a young man standing in front of one of his sex shops with a woman whom I assumed had been his first wife.

The furniture was the same, but the chairs had been moved around from when I had been here last. Probably the cops. Maybe the murderer. Not unusual. My mind turned at the speed of light, trying to pick everything up, trying to figure out what the fuck happened because I had a very clear vision of how the cops could turn this on me.

"You have any suspects?" It came out of my mouth like I was a kid asking for ice cream.

Petrillo's eyes grew wide just enough that I noticed his interest in my question, as if he'd either been waiting for it, or not expecting it at all.

"What do you think?" he asked.

"I don't," I said. "You guys have more unsolved murders than any other department in the state. I'm just curious if this is going to be another notch on the department's record."

"That's bullshit, Vega. You know, I broke protocol letting you in here. You give me that crap."

"Get angry," I said. "But it's a fact. I'm just wondering if you have any ideas, clues, leads, whatever."

"We're looking into it."

One of the medical examiners took a photo and the flash filled the study with white light. It brought me out of my trance. I wasn't here to do a story for the paper. I had come to tell Nick about Maya. I was done.

The other detective came back into the study. He didn't look at us but nodded to one of the medical examiners. He put on a pair of blue gloves, and the two of them picked up the big penis and placed it in a plastic evidence bag.

"Come on." Petrillo raised his arms. "Let's give them some room."

Rachel, who had been mesmerized by the sexual paraphernalia and the guitar player for the Funky Donkeys, shook her head and led the way out of the study.

"So you got an ID on the body?" I was trying to sound tough, aloof.

"We're going to have to get that through fingerprints or dental records." Petrillo paused and looked at Rachel and me for a moment. Then he leaned closer. "It's probably Nick Zavala. It's his place. But don't print that."

Rachel leaned her weight on one leg. "Am I going to get a picture?"

Petrillo pointed to the side of the house. "That would be a good place. Stay out of the way. When they roll out the gurney with the body, you can snap a couple. That suit you okay?"

Rachel smiled. I nodded and walked out of the house with her. We stopped between one of the police cars and the house. She grabbed my arm. "So what's the gossip?"

"What?"

"You said you had something juicy for me."

I looked at her big brown eyes. They took amazing, powerful photographs. I was lost for a minute, my mind swimming in ideas of Nick Zavala, images of him opening the door to his house in his bathing suit, of him offering me a drink, cocaine, money. Of my hands all over the bronze sculpture.

"Dexter."

"I saw Holly," I said quickly. "She kissed me."

"Get out!"

Rachel loved drama, especially where it concerned Holly and me. Maybe she also had a crush on her. Why not? "But we were both a little drunk," I said.

"So what? True feelings reveal themselves when you're drunk."

"Yeah, except I've called and texted her five times today, and she won't answer me."

"Don't obsess. You do that. You obsess over shit all the time. You gotta give her some room."

"Didn't you tell me I had to show her I cared?"

"Yeah, but take it easy. Don't badger the woman. You're gonna freak her out."

I stabbed my chest with my thumb. "She's freaking me out."

"Man, you're going to fuck it up again. Let her hunger a little."

She looked behind me where the police line kept the small crowd back. "There's my reporter interviewing Petrillo." Then she looked at me. "What are you doing here, anyway?"

"Just passing by on my way to a friend's house."

"Bullshit. You don't have any friends."

I smiled and backed away. "We should get together sometime. Have a drink."

"Or a big bottle of Fireball." She laughed and ambled toward the house where Petrillo had told her to wait for the gurney.

I walked under the police tape and down the block to my car.

CHAPTER SEVEN

As I DROVE home, the severity of the situation sank in. My stomach ached. My hands were shaking. I needed a drink—something hard and messy and fast—Bourbon or Mezcal.

I stepped into the house and saw the mess. Everything had been disturbed, gone through, tossed, fucked with. The couch cushions had been pulled out, tossed on the floor. The fabric sliced. Books, clothes all over the place. Records—my precious vinyl—scattered like trash. The whole place was upside down.

I ran to the kitchen and pulled out my cookbooks. There it was. Between the pages of Diana Kennedy's book: the five grand.

The laptop. I froze for a moment trying to piece it together: all the moments of the last twenty-four hours raining down on me like rocks.

It was gone. They'd taken the laptop. But my stereo was there, untouched: an open-face vintage Scott 222c, the Thorens 160, B&W speakers. All together they could fetch over a grand, maybe two. That was a lot of money in my world. They hadn't touched the TV either. Just the laptop.

I dropped on the desk chair. Mimi came out from somewhere in the mess, strutting her stuff. She hopped on the couch and stretched and yawned like nothing was wrong. Well, that was that. At least I hadn't been pummeled to death like Nick Zavala. All the money in the world was useless wherever he was now.

I took a long, deep breath, pushed myself off the chair, and went to the cupboard by the fridge. In the very back I found an old bottle of tequila, shitty stuff whose name, Grande Sombrero, didn't even make any sense. Probably 30 percent agave, 70 percent rotgut. It had two shots left. I put them down like a college kid on Cinco de Mayo.

I plopped down on the bare couch, my ass sinking deep between the broken springs. I ran everything through my faulty brain, every damn detail I could think of, but I couldn't see a blip. Nothing. Why would someone want my laptop?

It was a four-year-old MacBook Pro. Not worth much. The stereo—the records—were worth at least five times as much. My computer had addresses, my e-mail inbox, the research from my stories for the last four years, and the drafts of the stories for *Sarasota City Magazine*.

What really got me was my e-mail in-box. I had a lot of data, a lot of conversations in there. It made me nauseous just to think someone, some fucking criminal, had access to my personal life, my past—e-mails between my ex-wife and me, Holly and me. I rushed to the bathroom and gave everything back to the toilet. I sat on the floor, arm draped over the commode. It wasn't just the burglary, but the whole thing: getting laid off, Nick's murder. And Holly.

I closed my eyes and tried to think of the good old days, of sitting back in the newsroom, the phone hanging on my shoulder, believing the world was anxiously awaiting my next hard-hitting piece. I had been so sure of myself. I was the first one in my family to go to college. My parents had their own story of struggle—children of Mexican immigrants who came to this country during WWII and worked in the fields and factories. My sister and I were raised by my mother. But what left me with a chip on my shoulder, that anger that motivated me to become a journalist, to kick ass hard and hold nothing back, had nothing to do with them. Everyone struggles. It was my father and what happened to him—what I witnessed that summer day in 1980 made me who I became. It was the lone reason why I couldn't fail.

Now I was a fucked-up has-been unemployed reporter for a small-town paper. All the hard work, the anger, the resolution, the desire, the accomplishments—it had all been for nothing. I was as good as my dying father on that lone stretch of asphalt outside San Antonio, Texas.

A noise out front startled me out of my misery. I struggled to stand.

I heard the front door open and the screen door slam shut. "Dex?"

"Holly?"

I washed my face, rinsed my mouth.

"What's going on, Dex?"

I stumbled out of the bathroom. Holly was standing in the middle of the living room. She was perfect, too perfect. Totally out of place. She didn't belong here, in this pathetic mess. And I could tell she could see it. It was crystal clear from her expression. She was disgusted.

But she was sweet. She caressed my cheek. "Are you okay?"

"I'm fine."

"What are you, spring cleaning?"

"Not me," I said. "Someone broke in."

"You're kidding."

"I wouldn't treat my records like this."

"My God, Dex. Did you call the police?"

"Not yet."

"Did they take anything?"

"Just my laptop."

"You going to report it?"

"I don't know. Maybe." I took her arm and walked her slowly over the debris to the couch. "First thing in the morning."

She stared at the mess. "It's worth a try. But they rarely recover stolen goods. Statistics—"

"I know, I know. It's a one in a million. It was probably some crack head who's going to try and pawn it somewhere."

"You have a serial number?"

"I got it somewhere, I'm sure."

"Dex." I could see the pity over her green eyes. "I'm worried about you."

I was down, a little buzzed, confused. My mind was twirling. I wanted to crawl into the bottom of the couch, disappear.

"I waited for you at Michael's on East," she said. "What happened?"

"I left you a dozen voice mails. You never responded."

She smiled, but it looked forced. "I never got a message, Dex. I tried calling you like an hour ago."

I pulled out my phone. There it was, a missed call from a number I didn't recognize.

"But, I called," I mumbled and pressed buttons into my phone. I showed her the calls.

"That's my old number, silly."

She was nice enough to help me clean up a bit, pick up the records and clear a path to the bedroom. She fed Mimi and made some tea, which tasted like shit. Then she told me we'd get together another time.

It hurt, not because she left or because she saw me like this, but because she felt sorry for me. It was like a dagger in my heart.

* * *

In the morning I shook off all the depressing shit from the previous night and met the merciless Florida sun with a big smile. True. Nothing had changed as far as my life was concerned, but I hadn't gotten drunk for the first time since I was laid off from the paper. I slept a solid ten hours. The clarity with which I processed reality was phenomenal.

I cleaned the house. But I didn't just put things back in their place. I cleaned the shit out of the place, so by late afternoon it looked like a feature in *Architectural Digest*.

I still had to deal with the two articles I had pending for *Sarasota City Magazine*. They were due in a few days, but my drafts were in my laptop. I wasn't sweating the articles. They were brainless fodder for people who liked to read about themselves. There was nothing special about the places I was writing about. They were just like all the other McMansions in town, decorated by a hired hack who filled the rooms with so much crap they looked like displays.

I knew I could wing the articles. I just had to get another computer, sit tight for a few hours, and spill it. All I had to do was load the copy with adjectives and adverbs and gush about the beauty and originality of the place. The editor would love it, and I would get my check.

I drove north to the computer store that's just past the airport. But as I passed the art school, I couldn't help veering off the Trail and taking Bay Shore Road. I told myself I was only taking the scenic route, but the truth was that I was curious. I wanted to see what was going on around Nick's place.

There was a police cruiser and an unmarked police car, a white Grand Marquis, in the driveway. They were still investigating. It set off a small alarm in the back of my head. The cops were not just going to let this one fall off the radar. Or maybe they had no suspects and needed to find one. Anyone.

I turned the corner and pulled up a few yards ahead of the house so I could sit and watch the action through the rearview mirror. I was curious to see who was leading the charge: Petrillo or the new guy.

It wasn't long before a uniformed officer walked out to his cruiser. He grabbed a black case from the trunk and walked back in the house. Maybe it was routine, but it looked off. The cops seemed to have real purpose, going above and beyond for old Nick.

When I switched my glance, I noticed a teenage girl standing on the other side of the street ahead of me. She was staring at Nick's house. She was blond, barefoot, and wore cutoff jean shorts and a pink tank top.

She stood with her arms crossed, slightly hidden from Nick's house by a couple of small palms. It was pretty obvious what she was doing. Then it hit me: the topless girl taking in the sun by the pool when I visited Nick that day. Her eyes shifted back and forth from the house to the street. She looked impatient, scared, shifting her weight from one leg to the other, biting her fingernail.

I got out of the car and walked to the end of the block. I didn't look at her, but I could tell she was watching me. I crossed the street to her corner. She fidgeted, turned away.

"How's it going?"

She glanced at me and shrugged. Then she looked ahead at Nick's house.

"You remember me?" I said.

"What are you talking about?"

"At Nick's house a couple days ago."

She dropped her arms to her sides. "I ain't never seen you before in my life."

"Maybe not," I said. "But I saw you hanging out by the pool. Naked."

There was movement in front of Nick's house. The uniformed cop walked out. He got in his cruiser, but didn't drive away.

"They're looking for clues," I said.

She turned her eyes toward me.

Looking at her now, up close, she appeared to be fifteen, maybe sixteen. She was pretty, but rough around the edges, baby fat filling her chin and cheeks. It was obvious life had toughened her up. Like a runaway. On the back of her shoulder she had a colorful tattoo of a butterfly.

"Oh yeah?"

"They're trying to figure out who killed Nick," I said.

"I don't know nothin' about that."

I smiled. "You a neighbor?"

"Sort of."

"You don't live around here, do you?"

She laughed and pointed to a large obnoxious mansion three houses down on the next block. "I live in that big house over there. My daddy's a big-time lawyer. He's pals with the mayor. So fuck off."

"It must be nice," I said.

"What the fuck you want?"

"You're Nick's friend. Cindy, right?"

She took a step back, looked me up and down. "You a cop?"

"Do I look like one?"

She shrugged and turned her gaze back to Nick's house. The young detective from last night—Frey—had just walked out. He had a small plastic bag with him. He checked in with the policeman in the cruiser and then got in his Grand Marquis. They both drove off.

As soon as the cars were out of sight, Cindy started toward Nick's house.

I grabbed her arm. She tore way. "Hands off, creep!"

"What happened to Nick?"

"What do you think happened? Someone broke in and beat the shit outta him."

"Who?"

"How the fuck should I know?"

"Did you see him?"

"I didn't see shit."

She started for the house again. I walked after her. "Look, Cindy—"

"It's Tiffany, you dumb ass."

"Right. Tiffany."

She went right up to the house, raised the police's plastic yellow do-not-cross tape, and tried the door. It was locked. She turned around and looked past me at the street.

"What's going on?"

"I gotta get my shit."

She looked to the left and right then made her way around the house. There was a wall about seven feet high with a gate without a latch, only a handle. It opened from the inside. She looked around like she was lost.

Then she gestured at me with a wave of her hand. "Help me up."

"What?"

"Help me over."

"No." This was an active crime scene. Crossing it was a felony. If we got busted, we could become suspects. If they heard my voice mail, found my prints, I would be on Petrillo's radar. I was not going to give them any help.

Tiffany waved me over and stomped her foot like a bratty child. "Come on, man."

I stepped back from the gate and shook my head. "If you didn't kill Nick, you have nothing to worry about."

"Fuck Nick. I need my stuff."

"You can't do this. It's illegal."

"If you help me, I'll tell you everything I know."

I walked to the gate, stared at her.

She bit her lip. "I swear."

I took a deep breath, laced my fingers together, and leaned over, offering her a step. She placed one of her dirty bare feet in my hands. I hoisted her up. She placed her other leg up on the wall and pushed herself over.

She didn't open the gate. I pulled the handle. "Hey, open up."

I heard her walking away. I jumped up, pulled myself up—no easy feat—and rolled over the wall to the other side.

Tiffany was already by the wall of sliding glass doors. She tried one after the other, cursing after each one until she came to the last one. When that one didn't open, she looked back at the pool, at me, at the wall of glass. She backed up, picked up a carved rock ashtray from one of the patio tables, stomped back to the glass door.

I yelled: "No!"

She threw the ashtray. It hit the glass door and bounced right back and hit her in the face. She stumbled back, brought her hands to her face.

"What the fuck?" she yelled through her hands. She was looking down, blood dripping from her nose on to the stone patio. All I could think of was: evidence.

"They're impact resistant," I said. "For hurricanes."

She looked at me, wiped her nose with the back of her hand. Then she pulled the handles of the sliding glass doors back and forth like a frustrated child.

She was crazy. And I had no business risking jail time. I owed nothing to Nick Zavala. It was just curiosity.

"Tell me what you know," I said. "What happened to Nick?"

She looked at me like I was insane. But I could see in her eyes that she was out of it. Her pupils were dilated. "Fuck you."

"Hey," I said. "I helped you over the wall."

"Help me get inside," she said and pointed at the glass doors.

"No. That wasn't the deal. What happened?"

"Go to hell," she cried and then screamed in frustration, her arms flailing like she was swatting a swarm of bees around her head.

I tried. That was that. It was time to leave. The cops could be coming back any minute. I wasn't going to be caught behind police lines, in a crime scene with some psycho whose fingerprints were all over the house.

I flicked the latch on the gate and walked quickly back to my Subaru. The whole way to the computer store, I kept telling myself that Tiffany knew nothing. She was bluffing. That she was just someone who knew Nick. Whoever she was, she wasn't reliable. And besides, it wasn't my job to find the murderer. I wasn't a cop. I wasn't writing a story. I was done with it.

CHAPTER EIGHT

I DROPPED A grand for a new laptop and went home to write my two stories for *Sarasota City Magazine*. These stupid articles hung over me like a prison sentence. I wouldn't be free until I got them done. I had to focus, get them done, and find work. I needed a job.

I wrote the articles from memory. I described the houses, invented quotes from the owners, and peppered the whole thing with fancy adjectives like quaint, elegant, rich, sparkling, magnificent. Then I went on the attack with adverbs like calmly, boldly, utterly, and surprisingly. When I was done, I had the word count I needed. Both articles were masterpieces in shit writing. But I was done. I was free. I attached the files to an e-mail, addressed it to the editor, and clicked send.

In the early evening the sky turned gray with rain clouds. I popped open a cold beer and sat on the front porch.

My mind drifted back to Nick. I couldn't let go of it. Why did Tiffany have such an urgent need for her things? What were her things?

She looked like she was half homeless. Maybe Nick had taken her in, cleaned her up, given her money. Maybe he was fucking her. Probably. But I was pretty sure she hadn't killed him. I couldn't see that skinny teenager swinging that giant bronze penis, whacking him repeatedly in the head. No. She was tough, but she wasn't strong enough. That dick was heavy.

The cops had said there was no forced entry. It had to be someone he knew. But I had no clue who Nick knew. He had offered
me coke that day at his house. Who knew what kind of shit he was
involved in. Maybe he owed someone money. Or maybe he pissed
off his dealer. And then there was the rough guy at the bar. I don't
know.

* * *

When I finished my beer, I drove back to Nick's place to see what
was going on.

The cops were there. Again. Two cruisers and an unmarked white
Grand Marquis. Probably the same one that had been there earlier
in the day. I drove past. Maybe Tiffany had managed to get inside,
grabbed her stuff, and split. It brought a smile to my face when I
thought of her getting away with her shit. And maybe a nice original painting, an Andy Warhol or Peter Max she could sell on eBay
and live happily for the rest of her life.

I came around the block and went home. On the way I stopped
at the liquor store, bought a bottle of Don Julio and a twelve of
Darwin's Summadayze IPA.

When I got home there was a late-model red VW Beetle convert-
ible parked in the driveway. I parked beside it and walked slowly
around the side to the front porch. I found Holly pacing back and
forth, one arm over her chest, her hand tucked under her armpit,
the other hand holding her phone to her ear. She wore her hair
down. Her red lips seemed to glow in the late afternoon light.

When she saw me walk up, she spoke quickly into the phone:
"—I'll call you back."

"This is a nice surprise." I set the box of beer on the side table.

"Dexter." She put her phone away and hugged me. "I've been waiting for you for an hour."

She smelled so nice. "Did we have a date?"

I unlocked the door and let her in. I put the booze on the kitchen counter. When I turned, she was looking the place over.

"You cleaned up," she said. "I don't think I've ever seen your house look this good."

"Yeah, the maid finally showed up after five years."

She smiled. "I'm glad to see you still have a sense of humor."

"Always. Want a drink?"

"No thanks. Did you report the robbery?"

"Not yet."

"What about your laptop?"

"I got a new one."

"That was fast," she said and tossed her pretty blond hair to the side.

I popped open a beer and leaned against the threshold and looked at how beautiful she was. The last three years had done her a world of good. Or maybe it was the separation from Joaquin, Justice for All, del Pino.

"So what's up?" I said. "I don't see you in three years and suddenly you show up at my house twice in two days."

"Dex," she said and glanced at the ground where Mimi had just trotted past on her way outside. Then she raised her eyes. She was serious as a bullet. "Leslie, my paralegal, was at the police station today. She said she overheard Petrillo and Frey talking about you."

"Hey, I'm famous."

"I'm not joking, Dex. They talked about you in terms of being a suspect . . . in a murder."

"What?"

She averted her eyes. "Leslie said they were making fun of you. That they had your prints on . . . on a giant penis."

I laughed. The irony, the humor—the seriousness of their bullshit. I took a long drink of beer and plopped myself down on the sofa. I had worried about Tiffany when I should have been worried about me.

"It was a sculpture," I said. "It wasn't a real penis, it was a sculpture."

"Jesus, Dex. Forget the penis. What's going on?"

I told her I had helped Nick home from Memories. That he had invited me in for a drink and that was it. He had been showing off his art collection and had asked me to pick up the big penis sculpture. I told her nothing about our business deal. And I certainly didn't mention Maya.

"Dex, Leslie says they're going to the State Attorney. They're going to get a warrant. If they—"

"They can't charge me. Or at least they can't convict me. I didn't know the man. And I had no motive."

"What are you talking about? Rich man is murdered in fancy bayside neighborhood. This is Sarasota. You know the cops. They might let murders in Newtown go unsolved, but not in Sapphire Shores. That's a whole different story. And if you're the only suspect—"

"You think I'm guilty?"

"No. But you know how they are."

I stood, took her in my arms, brought her close. "You're worried about me."

She pushed me away. "Of course I am. God, Dex. Think."

"It's going to be fine," I said, but really, it wasn't. I knew what she meant. The cops could go after me if they thought they could make it stick. My prints were on that stupid penis sculpture. They could invent a motive. They probably couldn't get me on murder one, but two, manslaughter. They had options. The prints could place me in the house with the murder weapon.

But I wasn't going to show Holly I was worried, scared. Fuck that. No more poor Dex. No more pity party. I was no candy-ass lawyer type. I was Dexter fucking Vega.

* * *

Nothing happened with Holly. She wept, told me how worried she was, and asked me to stay in touch. Then she left because she had a date, a dinner appointment with a client.

The minute she was gone it hit me hard. If Petrillo and Frey were serious about charging me, I had to find out what was going on. But I had no access to their files, to the house, evidence. I drove to Siesta Key to see Mike Boseman. Maybe he knew Nick or knew someone who knew Nick. Either way, at the moment he was my only lead.

I pulled up to his driveway, but something was different. The Jaguar was either gone or parked in the garage. I went up the steps and knocked on the door. No answer. I went around back. All the windows and glass doors were covered with hurricane shutters, locked in place. The hammock and the cushions for the iron patio furniture were gone. The place looked as if it had been locked up for the summer.

An elderly couple sat on the patio of the house next door, drinking cocktails, enjoying the sunset. I walked to the property line and called out, "Excuse me, have you guys seen Mike around?"

They looked at each other, then the woman said, "Who?"

"Mike Bosemean, your neighbor."

"Ah, he go in morning." She had a slight Russian accent. "He pack up. Taxi come get him."

"Do you know where he went?"

She shook her head. "I don't know this man."

* * *

I went home and paced around the house, downing beer after beer. I told myself not to touch the tequila. I had to keep it together, stay clear. I needed to think.

Someone had killed Nick and the only thing I knew for sure was that it hadn't been me. I should have stuck with Tiffany. Maybe she did know something after all. Or maybe the cops nabbed her and were going to make her the fall guy. Maybe she ratted me out. They could've showed her my picture. I could see her already, pointing at it with her skinny little fingers: "Yeah, that's him, Officer."

I called a friend at the department, Officer John Blake. He'd helped me out before when I was working on stories about the police culture of covering up for each other. He was my anonymous—my Deep Throat.

I caught him on his cell and gave him the skinny on what I knew about Nick Zavala and what I was looking for, but kept out a few details for my benefit. Just in case.

He laughed. "I can't just go into the file. It's not my case, Vega."

"I'm not asking you to go in the file," I said. "Just ask around. There can't be that many murder investigations going on in Sarasota."

"Not my department. You know that."

"You know that fat cop with the gap between his front teeth?"

"Gasanov?"

"Yeah, I think so. Big guy."

"Yeah, yeah."

"He was there. Petrillo and Frey have the case—"

"Frey's an asshole."

"I know. So's Petrillo when it really comes down to it."

"Okay," he said, "so, Gasanov."

"Right. Just ask him. See what he knows about this thing."

"How are you involved in this, Vega?"

"I'm not."

"Right."

"I'll never ask you for another favor again for as long as I live. Scout's honor."

I hung up with Blake, got another beer, and started a new Maya document on the computer. I laid it all down in chronological order, the whole enchilada: the rough guy at the bar, Tiffany, Maya. I left nothing out. Then I read it over to see if anything hit me. I needed a lead. I needed something to point me in the right direction.

I got bupkis.

CHAPTER NINE

A LOUD KNOCK on the door woke me up at seven forty-five in the a.m. I rolled out of bed, went to the door in pajama bottoms, no shirt. I was hoping for Holly. I got Petrillo and Frey.

"Can we come in?" Petrillo said.

I moved aside. They ambled in, their eyes working over my place.

"What's going on?" I asked.

Petrillo put his hands on his waist and puffed out his chest like a turkey. "You knew this guy Nick Zavala, didn't you?"

"Why do you ask?" Frey was touching the papers on my desk. "Bills," I said. "Nothing but bills."

"Why didn't you tell me you knew him when we were at the house?" Petrillo asked.

Frey picked up a small framed photograph of Zoe when she was in the first grade. "This your daughter?"

"Don't touch my shit," I said. "Or you can wait outside."

He raised his hands and stepped away from my desk. "So tell us about Nick," he said.

"I met the guy at a bar. He got into fisticuffs with some guy—"

"What guy?"

"Some drunk, I guess. So I gave him a ride home. That's all I know."

"What did he look like?"

"Who?"

"The drunk," Petrillo said. "Describe him for us."

"Average hight and build. Dirty blond hair. Looked like an un-employed construction worker."

"What was the argument about?"

"Nothing. Guy was drunk, angry. Took it out on the old guy."

"What bar was it?" Petrillo said.

"I forget," I lied. I wanted to check that out myself. "I was drunk."

Frey grinned. "And you drove?"

I offered him my wrists. "You gonna charge me with a DUI?"

"We're gonna charge you with murder one." Frey smiled like that whiny kid in the playground everyone hates.

"What have you two been smoking?" I said, and walked over to the kitchen. I opened myself a beer. "Either of you dildos want one?"

"We're on duty," Petrillo said.

I took a long swig of the Summadayze and smiled. "I'm not."

"Come on, Vega." Frey got in my face. I could smell the garlic in his breath. "You knew the guy. Maybe you two got in an argument. Maybe you got angry, lost your temper—"

"Call off your dog, Detective."

"Frey."

Frey waved a finger in my face. "We're on to you, Vega."

"He doesn't like me," I said, and pointed my beer at Petrillo.

"Neither do I," Petrillo said. "If you have anything to say, Vega, say it now. I don't want to have to come back with a court order, tear up your place. Make it easy on yourself."

"You're telling me I'm a suspect?"

Petrillo and Frey glanced at each other. "A person of interest," Petrillo said. His tone came down. He stepped back. He knew I wasn't going to give him shit for free.

Frey set his card on my desk. "If your memory comes back and you remember the name of the bar—or anything else for that matter—give us a ring. We like people who cooperate. We treat them nice."

"Tell me something," I said, and pointed at Frey but looked at Petrillo. "What carnival did you pick him up at?"

"Do me a favor," Petrillo said as he moved toward the front door. "Don't disappear."

"You know where to find me, Officer."

I watched them both walk out, the back of their broad shoulders, no necks, perfect hair followed by the smell of Paco Rabanne. I hated that cologne.

*   *   *

I called my lawyer, Brian Farinas. Technically, he was not my lawyer, but a friend who also happens to be a criminal attorney. I told him of my encounter with the dynamic duo.

"And?" he said.

"And what?"

"Are you guilty?" he said quickly like a lawyer running out of time. "Did you—"

"What the fuck kind of question is that?"

"It's *the* question, okay? I ask it of all my clients when they're being charged—"

"I'm not being charged."

"Not yet, you're not. But you might, right? I need to ask, Dexter. And you need to answer."

"I didn't kill him."

He sighed. "Good. Good. Very good."

It pissed me off, as if he might've thought I could be capable of murder. Maybe I needed to find a new lawyer friend.

"Just chill. Don't tell them anything. If they arrest you, call me. Don't tell them anything. Nothing. Keep your mouth shut."

"Got it."

"Nothing."

"I got it. Nothing."

"You haven't told them anything, right?"

When I didn't answer, he sighed. "You talked to them."

"A little."

"Well, no more. You have the right to remain silent. Live it, okay?"

"Yessir."

"Now, is there anything that can tie you to the murder?"

"I don't know. Maybe. Holly told me her paralegal overheard the detectives mention that my prints were on a sculpture."

"What sculpture? What are you talking about?"

"The murder weapon."

"He was killed with a sculpture?"

"Beat his head to a pulp."

"And your fingerprints are on it? Jesus, Dexter, that's not good. Do you have an alibi that can be corroborated? Someone who can vouch for you?"

"That would depend on when exactly he got killed." I told him how I'd left a message on Zavala's voice mail. "These things have a time on them. That will show I wasn't there."

"Don't be an idiot, Dexter. You could have been standing over the body when you made that call. It proves nothing. We need bodies, people who can say they saw you at the time of the murder in such and such a place."

There was Boseman and Holly and the AC repairman, but we didn't know the exact time of the murder. It was fifty-fifty—or less. Still, Brian dismissed the whole thing. "Well, there's no point in worrying about it until they charge you. We'll have plenty of time to prepare your defense."

"You seriously think they'll arrest me?"

"Frankly? I have no fucking idea."

* * *

Frey and Petrillo's little visit gave me the lead I needed: the bartender at Memories. It was a long shot, but it was all I had. Besides, I could also use a drink.

It was still early when I got there. I took a stool at the bar and asked Mac for a beer. When he came back and set the bottle in front of me, I asked him about Nick by name.

He looked toward the jukebox like he was thinking. "Can't say it rings a bell."

"Old guy, maybe mid-sixties. Rich."

Mac shook his head.

"He was here a couple days ago. Some tough guy tossed him out of the bar and started whaling on him—"

"Right. Right."

"That's the guy."

He waved a finger at me. "You know you guys never paid your bill that night."

I set a fifty on the counter. "Keep the change."

He took the cash, folded it, and placed it in his shirt pocket. "Yeah, that old guy. He comes in here every now and then, has a couple of drinks and leaves. I don't remember him talking to anyone, just keeps to himself. You know how it is. But I wouldn't call him a regular."

"You know anything about him?"

"Drank bourbon."

"Anything else?"

"Drove a nice Lexus."

"That's it?"

"That's it."

I drank my beer and ordered another. "What about that guy who was beating up on him?"

He shook his head. "Never saw him before or since. It happens. We get drifters and crack heads come in here and harass the customers. It's the neighborhood."

I finished my beer and walked to the door. Just as I was about to leave, I stopped, went back to the bar. "What about a girl," I said. "Tiffany."

Mac stared at me like he was really making an effort.

I held my hand up level with my shoulder. "About yay high, blond. Teenager, I think. Wears cutoffs and goes around barefoot. Kind of dirty, if you know what I mean?"

He shook his head. "I see a lot of people, man."

"Has a tattoo of a butterfly on her shoulder."

His eyes bounced. "Wait a minute, yeah. I think I know who you're talking about. She used to come in here every now and then, trying to hit up customers for a drink. I had to chase her out a couple of times. But that was months ago."

"You know where she lives?"

He shook his head.

I pulled out one of my business cards and wrote a note on the back: *I got your stuff from Nick's place. Call me.*

I handed it to Mac. "If she comes in here, can you give her this for me?"

"Sure."

I gave him a twenty. "And let her use your phone."

* * *

IT WAS DARK when I left the bar. I drove across the Trail and took Bay Shore to check out Nick's house. The white Grand Marquis was there. I kept going.

When I pulled into my driveway, there was another white Grand Marquis parked on the street in front of the house. Maybe this was it. The arrest. I thought of Brian Farinas. Say nothing.

Detective Petrillo and his right-hand asshole were sitting on the chairs on the front porch of my house.

"There he is," Petrillo said. He put down the magazine he'd been looking at and stood. "Where you been, Dexter?"

"Looking for a job. Thought I'd check in with the police department. I heard they hire anyone off the street. No experience necessary."

"Nice." Petrillo shoved his hands in his pockets and walked away toward the Grand Marquis. I watched him go. I didn't know why I had played it tough. I guess I was pissed. It just came out of me at the sight of them invading my space.

Frey stood, pulled his jacket back, and set his hands on his waist revealing the handle of a silver-plated revolver tucked in a holster at his side. It was a big .44 or a .357. Not Sarasota PD's standard-issue Glock 40. "You got anything to say to me?" he said.

"Yeah," I said. "Fuck you."

He threw a hook. Caught me high on the gut. Blew my air. My knees buckled. He held me up and hooked me again, same place, knew exactly where to punch. Dropped me like a sack of mulch. I rolled to my side, curled up in a fetal position, gasping.

"Why don't you come by the office tomorrow and make a full confession," Frey said and kicked me in the side. Everything went black.

* * *

When I woke up, I was lying on the couch, my head resting comfortably on a woman's lap. I took in the sweet smell of my favorite perfume and smiled. Before I even opened my eyes, I knew it was Holly.

"Better?" she said.

I nodded.

"What's going on, Dex?"

"I don't know," I said. "Cops used me like a punching bag."

Holly chuckled. "Cops don't do that. It's against the law."

"Well these two did."

"Come on. Is it possible you came home drunk again?"

I sat up. "What are you talking about? They were waiting for me outside the house. They want something out of me."

"So why don't you tell them?"

"Tell them what?"

"Why don't you tell them what's going on, Dex. Or tell me. Maybe I can help."

I shook my head and took a deep breath. My stomach felt better, painful, but I could breathe easy. I got my bearings. Holly looked as beautiful as ever, red lips, green eyes, and all the empathy in the universe. "Why are you here?"

She frowned. "You want me to leave?"

"No. No." I got up and gestured for her to stay seated. I made my way to the kitchen and pulled out the last two beers. I put one on the table in front of her. "I think they want me to make a confession. That I killed Nick Zavala."

"That's ridiculous," she said. "That's not how the police work. If they don't have enough evidence, there's nothing they can do."

"Maybe they have no other leads. Petrillo's climbing the ladder. He wants Chief Miller's job. You know that."

"Well, he's not going to get it by abusing innocent people."

I raised my beer. "Here's to the idealist lawyers of the world."

"Dexter, I'm serious."

"So am I." I took a long drink and sat beside her. "How come you're here, Holly? I haven't seen you in who knows how long, and then here you are picking me up from the gutter. What's up?"

She stared at me with those bewitching green eyes. She caressed my hair. "I'm worried about you, Dex."

"I'm fine."

"No," she said. "I don't think so. The rumor around the courthouse is the State Attorney wants this resolved. The neighborhood is worried there's some psycho out there. They think they're going to be next. They have your prints on the murder weapon. Now you're telling me the police are trying to get a confession out of you."

"Yeah, but I didn't do it. And they don't have a motive."

"They have a voice mail. You told Nick you were on your way. You know they'll make a case out of it, Dex. I don't want you to go to jail."

It was nice to feel loved, even if it had to be under these circumstances. I touched her shoulder and moved closer. She stood.

"Dex," she said. "We need to do something about this."

"We?"

"You. Whatever. I'll help you. Just tell me what happened. How do you know this man, Zavala?"

"I told you."

"There has to be more to it than that. Why were you going to his house that night?"

"I don't know," I said. "I need to think."

"Dex. You need to trust me."

"I do. I trust everybody. That's my problem."

Then my phone rang. It was Nancy, my ex-wife. I looked at Holly and held my phone up. "I have to take this."

She gave me a look.

"You didn't call," Nancy said, skipping formalities and getting right to the point.

"Something came up." I was supposed to talk to Zoe. We talked every week. She told me about school and her friends and asked me when I was going to see her again. It was always the same. And every time it broke my heart because there was nothing I could do except tell her I'd see her soon. But soon was an eternity for a seven-year-old girl. It was an eternity for me.

"Something always comes up," Nancy said. "You'd think you could make a little time for her. You don't see how disappointed she is when you don't answer. You need to get your priorities straight."

"I'll talk to her next week. I—"

Holly glanced at her watch. "I have to go," she mouthed.

"Call her tomorrow morning," Nancy said. "I told her you would."

"What about school?" I said and gestured for Holly to wait.

"She has a cold. I'm keeping her home. Call her."

She hung up. I glanced at my phone. I had a voice mail.

Holly took my arm. "I have to let my dogs out. I'll try and come back later."

I moved close to her. She squeezed my arm, smiled, gave me the look. We drew close, kissed.

She walked quickly toward the door. Then she stopped and turned to face me. "Dex, be careful."

I stood in the middle of the living room, a beer in my hand and the taste of her tongue in my mouth. I heard her car start, back out of the driveway, and drive off.

I played the voice mail in my phone. It was Zoe. *Hi, Daddy. Mommy said I could call you because you didn't call. I'm sick. Mommy says I have a fever. I have to tell you about my art project. I made a painting of you and me at the beach and it won a prize at the school show. I wanted to give it to you, but Mommy's friend Zach said he really liked it and Mommy said I should give it to him so he can hang it in his office. Also, I want to get a puppy, but Mommy said I can't have one. Maybe you can talk to her and tell her it's a good idea. Okay? I love you, Daddy.*

Hearing Zoe, her innocence, the simplicity of her requests, her generosity, broke my heart. I was a terrible father. She didn't deserve me. I set my empty beer down, took Holly's, and guzzled it.

I couldn't stand feeling so damn helpless, made my stomach turn. Zoe was in Texas with her mom, and there was nothing I could do about it. The whole system is rigged. The kids are always the losers when it comes to divorce. Nancy put up a good fight with a good lawyer. It broke me financially and emotionally. But that was five years ago. I had to trust that Zoe knew better. That I loved her and wanted to be with her, but there were forces greater than us that prevented me from making her life as perfect as I wanted it to be.

I paced. I pushed my thoughts of Zoe out of the way and concentrated on Zavala. I had to figure it out. I had to clean up the mess.

I opened my Maya file. I added all the info from the last day, every detail, even the beers I drank at Memories and the cash I gave Mac. Then I leaned back on my chair and reviewed everything.

I had a journalism professor at the University of Houston who said the most important thing when doing research for an article was to turn the facts around and look at the project from the opposite angle, use a different point of view, a different narrator.

I did that. I did it from every possible angle. But I still came up empty. The only thing I could figure was that Tiffany had the answer to the puzzle. Or maybe not. She could be in the exact same position I was in—an innocent bystander who got caught in the crossfire. And who knew? Maybe she was already in police custody, telling Petrillo and Frey everything, making up all kinds of stories.

But what if she wasn't in custody? I could cruise the North Trail and look for her. And if I found her, what then? It didn't mean shit. Besides, it could take me weeks or months to find her. Or the rough guy from Memories. No. Whoever killed Nick had access to the house. And a motive.

Then there was Maya. She and Tiffany knew Nick. They were the only ones who could help me figure this thing out and avoid getting nailed for Nick's murder.

I had Maya's information in my little notebook. I flipped through the pages. Colonia Roma. The biology team with the UNAM. It wouldn't be difficult to find her, just find the university team working with the salamanders in Xochimilco. She might know if Nick had any enemies. She'd have names of acquaintances, people I could interview, leads to possible motives.

Besides, in a strange way, I felt I owed it to Nick. He hired me to find his daughter. I hadn't completely fulfilled my job. And I still had about eight grand left of the money he'd paid me.

Yeah, I'm kind of honest that way.

CHAPTER TEN

I FLEW OUT of the Tampa airport with a brief layover in Houston. I called Zoe and did my best to convey my feelings, that I loved her more than my own life and that one day things would be different and we'd be together more often. My words seemed to fly over her head, although one never knows. She just said she understood that I was very busy, and made me promise I would talk to Nancy about the puppy. I laughed about the simple innocence of her world. I only wished it could stay that way forever.

Landing at night in Mexico City is like floating into a display of Christmas lights. The city goes on forever. The lights spread all over the valley and get lost among the mountains, then reappear on the side of a mountain and drift in patches down toward the valley—reds and yellows and whites—a magic constellation far off in a different galaxy.

My grandparents were Mexican, but I had only been to Mexico once, and my Spanish was rudimentary, if not worse. When I first visited the country three years ago, I went to the state of Jalisco to find the family of the migrant worker that had been shot and killed by a Sarasota police officer. I hired a fixer I found through a colleague who worked with the Associated Press in Miami. She called the Mexico City bureau, and they found me a young man, Fidel Prado. He took me to Jalisco, translated, and showed me the ins and outs of the intricacies of dealing inside Mexico. Fidel was great. But when I e-mailed him about helping me on this trip, he was unavailable. He now worked for the government's press and communications office and was up to his neck deflecting press inquiries about accusations of government corruption and the rumor that the president was directly involved in the disappearance of forty-three students in the southern state of Guerrero at the hands of the police. Still, Fidel agreed to set me up with a gringo journalist who knew the expat community in the city. It made sense. After all, I was looking for an American woman who'd been in Mexico City for a few months, not a family of peasants in the middle of nowhere.

I checked in to the Hotel Maria Cristina, a relatively inexpensive place in the financial center of the city. It was a throwback to the 1970s with clean but basic rooms. What it lacked in luxury, it had in the perfect bar, a small colonial-style cottage across a pleasant garden inside the hotel property. That little bar made you feel like you were really in Mexico. It had comfortable seats, a patio, bowls with salted peanuts, WiFi, and a heavyset, attentive bartender named Julio.

It turned out that the gringo Fidel had set me up with was not a gringo at all. Malcolm Stone was a high-strung Scotsman. He rolled his r's like an old diesel engine and spoke much too fast for me to understand what he said. I had to keep asking him to repeat everything, which pissed the hell out of him. He was young—early twenties, had a flat boxer's nose and messy pink-blond hair. He said he'd been struck by lightning when he was a teenager. It gave him a twitch that made him blink all the time as if he were suffering from shell shock.

I gave him the lowdown on Maya and the salamanders. "She's supposed to be working with a team from the university. But I don't know where she lives. I only have two locations: Xochimilco and Colonia Roma. And I don't have a lot of time."

He downed his third Negra Modelo and made a gesture with his hand for me not to worry. "We'll find her, not a problem. Mexico's big, but Mexico's small. You know what I mean?"

I didn't. But it wasn't exactly the conversation I wanted to have at the moment. I tossed a couple of peanuts into my mouth and said, "I need to start right away."

"Right, then. We'll start first thing in the morning. I'll come get ya, right? We'll go get lost in Xochimilco. A fine place to start. You'll fucking love it. Doesn't feel like you're in the city at all."

"What about this Colonia Roma?"

"That's a neighborhood, yeah? I'll ask around." He gestured for Julio to bring two more beers. "You need to meet Toni. I'll introduce you. Bloody socialite if I ever met one, Toni Spencer. She knows everyone. She lives in La Roma. Knows every fucking thing that goes on. And she's downright hot, too. Untouchable, but bloody hot."

It sounded like a good plan. Julio brought two more beers. Afterward, Malcolm and I walked a couple of blocks up the street where a man and a woman ran a little taco stand on the sidewalk outside a parking garage: three plastic tables and chairs and a small aluminum vat where they fried quesadillas stuffed with mushrooms, chiles, and squash blossoms and sausage.

Malcolm told me he'd been in Mexico four and a half years. He worked as a freelance journalist for a number of British and U.S. papers. He said the work was good. "But it's the fucking lifestyle. That's why I stay, right? I'm not getting rich, but who is?" He laughed a maniacal laugh. "I can't complain. Or I could. Yes, I could. But I bloody won't. Anyway, beats the fuck out of living in Scotland."

We parted ways in front of the hotel, agreeing to meet early in the morning and go to Xochimilco.

The following morning after I'd had breakfast, I stood alone outside the hotel door, watching the secretaries and young executives and office workers in their dark gray and blue suits walking to their jobs. About an hour later I got a text from Malcolm: *Can't make it. Minister of Energy resigned. Have to write story. Take taxi. Enjoy X. Meet for drinks after.*

The drive was long, complicated, and prolonged by traffic. On the way the driver gave me a colorful historical narrative of the place they call the floating gardens of Mexico. He explained that Xochimilco was the last vestiges of what had once been an intricate network of canals and man-made islands that dated back to the time of the Aztecs. They had been declared a UNESCO World Heritage Site, and Mexicans like himself enjoyed outings with family and friends on occasional Sundays. He was sure I would enjoy it, but he couldn't understand why I wanted to be there so early in the morning because things there really didn't get going until the afternoon unless it was a weekend.

I wondered about Maya. If I found her, what would I tell her? Would I even recognize her? Would she talk to me? And if she did, would she tell me about her father? Would she have a lead to people with possible motives for killing Nick?

Did she even know her father had been murdered?

The taxi driver dropped me off in the main tourist hub of Xochimilco. It was the end of a canal packed with flat-bottom boats with arched roofs and fancy facades painted and decorated with colorful flowers. There were dozens of them lined up one next to the other and one in front of the other. But there didn't seem to be anyone around.

It was quiet. There was a light fog, and the air was moist and stank of old vegetables and sewer. There was trash floating on the dark green water: candy wrappers, fruit peels, Styrofoam containers, empty cans.

I made my way along the water's edge. A little boy about eight years old came running up to me with his hand out. He was filthy, barefoot, wore dirty pants and a ripped sweater.

"*No me da un peso pa comer?*" He walked alongside of me, moving his hand from his mouth to his belly and out to me again. "Please, mister. *Cinco pesos.*"

I waved him away and kept walking. A scrawny brown mutt scurried past. Then a boy, about fourteen, appeared from behind an abandoned food stand and ran toward us waving a thin long cane.

I stepped back. He whacked the little kid. "*Andale cabrón, largate pinche puto!*"

The younger boy cowered and ran away. Then the older one turned to me and gave me a big smile. "Sorry, my friend. *Amigo.*"

I dropped my guard, took a deep breath.

"No problem," he said. "All good, no?"

"What's the matter with you?" I said. "He wasn't doing any harm."

He laughed. "No, no. He a very bad boy. He sniff glue." He tossed the stick and ran his index finger around his ear. "He no good. *Muy loco.*"

This boy didn't look much different than the kid he'd just chased off. The only difference was that he wore sandals. I looked past him at the canal where a man in a small wooden boat was approaching. The boy followed my gaze and smiled. "You want to take trip in a *trajinera?*"

"No," I said. "I'm looking for someone. A girl."

"Ah, you want girls. No problem. But they sleep now. Too early. Too much party last night."

I shook my head. "I'm looking for one person. A woman who's working with the university. She's looking for the salamander, the axo . . . axolotl."

The boy smiled and waved his hand from left to right. "No more axolotl. All dead. All gone."

"I know. But have you seen biologists, students?"

He smacked his chest with his hand. "I am Ernesto."

"Dexter."

"You come from the Estates?"

"That's right. And I'm looking for a friend who's working with a team from the university, with the UNAM. Do you know where they are?"

He looked at me as if I'd asked him if he'd been to the moon. Then he nodded and motioned for me to follow him. We approached the old man in the small wooden launch with a little motor that had been pulled from a scooter. He agreed to take me around for a few hundred pesos. Ernesto invited himself along. I couldn't tell if he was in business with the old man, or if he was just coming for the ride. Either way, I didn't mind.

It turned out Xochimilco was not simply a lake with a couple canals south of Mexico City. It was a town and a huge area with little lakes and a maze of canals peppered with small settlements along the banks. We wandered endlessly without apparent direction. In the morning fog, it had a creepy, ethereal feel—like we were stepping back in time.

"The islands are man-made. They're called *chinampas*." Ernesto pointed out the line of trees along the rectangular islands. "The people built the islands a long time ago. Very good soil for crops in the *chinampas*. Corn. Beans. Chile."

The old man sat quietly in the back of the little launch looking ahead, the engine puttering at a steady rhythm like an old lawn mower. Whenever Ernesto said something to him, he didn't smile or frown. He just nodded and kept on going, his little beady eyes focused somewhere in the fog.

We passed a few shacks and shanties. Great big trees grew along the sides of the canals, their canopy forming tall, natural tunnels. The deeper we went into the maze, the foggier it became. At times, we couldn't see more than thirty yards ahead.

The drone of the motor was making me drowsy. There was a slight chill in the air. I pulled up the collar of my jacket and closed my eyes. I breathed in the odd smell of the wet earth, pungent and sour. Then Ernesto nudged me. He pointed to one of the islands. The old man slowed the boat. It was like a mirage in the fog. Something was hanging on a tree. A head. An eyeless, hairless pink head the size of a cantaloupe.

As we got closer, I could see the island was covered in body parts: tiny plastic limbs and heads and fabric hanging from the trees and plants. Dolls tied to the branches, hanging, wrapped with rope to the trunk of the trees—heads, arms, legs. It was some creepy shit.

Ernesto smiled. "You like?"

"What is this?"

"*Isla de las Muñecas*," he said enthusiastically. The Island of the Dolls.

I remembered the post on Maya's Facebook. She had mentioned this place. We were getting close. I gave Ernesto a thumbs-up. "Are the biologists here?"

"The man he live here alone," Ernesto said. "He collect the dolls he find in the water. They say they come alive at night."

We drifted alongside the *chinampa*—mutant dolls everywhere.

"Don Julián, they say he see a girl die in the water. He put the dolls on the tree for her." Ernesto touched the side of his head with his index finger. "He say the dolls are her spirit. If you see, sometimes the dolls move. Look." He pointed at the trunk of a twisted juniper. It had doll heads all around it like a Christmas tree. But nothing moved.

"You see?" Ernesto said.

The old man crossed himself.

"Look, Ernesto. This is cool," I said. "But I need to find the biologists. Students looking for the axolotl. Help me out here."

He smiled and touched the old man's shoulder. Ernesto spoke, gesturing with his hands back and forth. The old man nodded and spoke with a deep voice.

Ernesto turned to face me, and nodded toward the old man. "Ausencio say he see students last week. But very far."

"How far?"

Ernesto waved. "Too far to go in his boat. You have to take car to San Lorenzo Atemoaya."

It took forever to get back to the dock where we had started. On the way, the fog began to lift. The landscape looked friendlier, the canals cleaner. I suppose it would have been enjoyable under other circumstances.

Ernesto came with me to the center plaza where we hired a taxi to take us to the neighborhood of San Lorenzo Atemoaya.

In Sarasota, waterfront property belongs to the rich. Here it was for the poor. Shanties made of block and wood and cardboard hung to the water's edge for as far as I could see. It was shack after shack after shack, ending at the canals. They had no sewer, but they'd dug narrow drainage ditches that carried the filth from the shacks to the waterways. It had to be poisoning whatever was supposed to live in the water: fish, frogs, the axolotl.

We got out of the taxi where the street ended at a crossroads with a muddy, unpaved road. We walked along the road, then took a narrow path that separated the shanties from the water. The foliage was lush and green. Between the shacks and the canal there were small yards with chickens and pigs. Clothes hung to dry. Women washed laundry by hand using concrete washboards.

We walked for almost an hour, leaving the town behind. The foliage became denser, the shacks more scattered. Then we came upon a turn in the path and found a camp at the water's edge.

Bingo.

Half a dozen young men and women were spread out in the grass, sitting cross-legged, writing on binders and clipboards. One of them was working on a laptop. There was a wooden launch tied to a young elm.

They all raised their eyes and watched us approach. One of the men, probably in his mid-twenties, stood and placed his hands on the sides of his waist. "*Buenos dias.*"

Ernesto introduced me as a gringo who was looking for the people trying to find the axolotl.

"You speak English?" I asked.

The man nodded and introduced himself as Roberto Magaña. "We're the research team with UNAM. How can we help you?"

"I'm looking for a woman," I said, looking past him, scanning the group for someone who might look like Maya. A person in a wet suit surfaced near the launch. "Her name is Maya Zavala," I continued. "She came here a few months ago from Florida to help search for the axolotl. Do you know her?"

Roberto shook his head and turned to his companions. "*Alguien conoce a una Americana que se llama* Maya Zavala?"

They shook their heads and looked at each other. Their eyes were blank, questioning.

I offered Roberto the photograph Nick had given me of Maya. "Are other teams working here? She could be with a different group or a different university."

"No," Roberto said flatly, still looking at the photo. "Not here. We've had a couple of American students come and help, but that was months ago. And they were men."

"No one else is searching for the axolotl?"

"I don't think so." He gave me back the photo. "We have a grant from the *Secretaría del Medio Ambiente* and support from the university. We're it. No one else cares for the axolotl."

I took a deep breath. Maybe Dr. Tabor and Boseman had been pulling my leg. I looked everyone over. They just sat in the grass looking at Ernesto and me, waiting. My eyes kept drifting back to the person in the wet suit and mask.

"You mind if my friend and I sit and take a break?" I was a little tired from the walk, but I also wanted to see who was behind the mask.

Roberto nodded and made a gesture for us to sit. "It's not our land. You're welcome to join us. I must apologize. This is very diffi-cult and frustrating work. We are all very tense."

"No sign of the little guys, huh?"

He shook his head.

"The axolotl is very important to Mexico." The person in the wet suit had pulled the mask off and was wading to shore. A woman. But it wasn't Maya. "People think it's just a salamander, a genetic freak of nature."

Her accent was heavy, but her English was good. She sat across from me and pulled the flippers off her feet. "The name axolotl is Nahuatl for water monster. It was what the Aztecs called it. Biologists breed them and study them because they have the ability to reproduce in the larvae stage and regenerate and grow any part of their body that is damaged."

"I wish I could do that."

She didn't find that funny. "But for Mexicans, this little amphibian represents something much greater. Like the canals of Xochimilco, they're what we have that remains of our culture before the Europeans destroyed it. They think they discovered us. But they're wrong. They've written their own history. Now we're writing ours. And the axolotl is at the core of our national identity. The Aztecs used it for medicinal purposes. It was very important to their culture. We be-lieve it is as much a key to our past as it is to the future of Mexico."

It sounded like hyperbole. I was thinking of two things: Maya Zavala, and this woman staring at me with a pair of amazing eyes that seemed to say that she couldn't give a damn whether I cared or not. She was covered in mud and algae while giving me this rant that was part ecological lesson, part politics, and part insult.

"I think it's a noble thing," I said, because I had absolutely no clue what to say. Flattery and the impression that I was on her side might help. She could know Maya. And I did care about nature. I cared that animals continued to live in the environment they had always inhabited. Except raccoons. I fucking hate raccoons.

She smiled and leaned to the side, resting her chin on her shoulder. "Everyone should have a purpose in life. The axolotl is ours."

"So if you find it, I suppose it will make the government take an interest and clean up this place."

"To hell with the government. They don't do anything for us. Do you know who lends us their boats? Who brings us lunch? Who gives us tips on where to search? The people who live here. The peasants who still grow crops in these little chinampas. They come with tortillas and stew and feed us and tell us stories of how they used to hunt the axolotl when they were children. They were everywhere then. No one thought they would disappear."

"I guess the city is encroaching in their habitat," I said.

"No one is happy about it. I think some of these people even feel guilty about it."

I looked at Ernesto. He nodded at me as if he understood and agreed and was ready to go to battle for this little reptile. The rest of the crew was back to work. Roberto was busy putting on a wet suit. The others were jotting down information on a map, taking notes, transcribing information into the laptop.

The woman introduced herself as Flor Quintero. Flor. Flower. I liked that right away. I asked her about Maya.

"Why are you trying to find her?" she asked. "Do you fear she has been kidnapped?"

"No. Or at least I don't think so."

"In Mexico, we walk with danger like it is our shadow."

It sounded a little melodramatic. But what did I know about living in Mexico? I offered her the photograph of Maya. "I don't think anything bad happened to her. It's just that her family has lost touch with her. Her father asked me to help him find her."

She studied the photo. When she looked at me again, I could see a slight change in her eyes. It was subtle. Maybe it was just a reaction to the light. She passed it back to me. "Are you a policeman?"

I laughed and shook my head. "I'm a reporter. A journalist. When I lost my job, Maya's father asked me to help. His last contact with her was about four months ago."

"That is a long time. Why did he wait so long to find her?"

It was a good question. "Maybe he was trying to give her a little space."

"Maybe she was fed up with her father's patriarchal ways."

"I don't know about that." She sounded as if she was talking of her own relationship with her father. "Well," I said, "things have gotten a little complicated in the last few days."

"Complicated, how?"

"Death in the family. That's why I came down here."

"I see." She wiped her face with a towel. "And you say she's a biologist?"

"Biology student. Her professor said she was obsessed with the axolotl."

She laughed a very deep, honest laugh. "We're all obsessed with the axolotl."

"That's why she came down here—to find it."

"And you thought she was working with us."

"That's what I was told. She was supposed to hook up with a team from UNAM."

"That is us."

I nodded. "So you see. It's a very intriguing case."

"Intriguing?" she said and smiled. She had a beautiful smile. "That is an interesting word to use."

"But it's true."

"The disappearance of the axolotl is an intriguing mystery."

"There you go." I laughed. I was thinking of what Dr. Tabor had said, that whoever finds an axolotl in its natural habitat will have their name written up in gold: biologist extraordinaire. "We have a lot in common. We're both searching for something."

"Yes," she said, "but at least for us, it will hopefully make a change in how we manage the lakes and canals of Xochimilco. And it can infuse the Mexican people with national pride. That is something we are in desperate need of—pride."

"*Disculpe, profesora,*" the young man on the launch said. "*Esta parte ya esta medida. Nos podemos mover al siguiente cuadrante?*"

I glanced at Ernesto.

Flor nodded at the young man and stood.

I stood and gave her my card. "I'm staying at the Hotel Maria Cristina. If you, or anyone, remembers her, or if you know of another group she might have worked with—"

"I told you."

"Please," I said. "I would really appreciate it if you got in touch."

She glanced at my card and back at me. "I must get back to work."

CHAPTER ELEVEN

WHEN I GOT back to my hotel in the late afternoon, I had a message from Malcolm to meet him at the Cantina Nuevo Leon in the Condesa neighborhood. When I got there he was already drunk. He admitted he'd lost my phone number and that he'd fucked up this morning, but that it couldn't be helped. He apologized and ordered a round of beers. "But the good news," he said in his muddy Scottish, "is that Toni Spencer's coming to meet us here. You can interrogate her to your heart's content. Right?"

We toasted with *caballitos* of 7 Leguas. Why you couldn't find this tequila in Sarasota was beyond me, but at least it was here. At least I was here. We drank, and Malcolm complained about Mexican politics and the insensitive and incestuous expat community, and about London United. By the time we toasted a fifth time, it was clear he harbored a deep resentment for everything under the sun.

Just as I was flying high, feeling like Spider-Man ready to swing between buildings, Toni Spencer walked in.

Toni wasn't exactly beautiful. She was attractive, elegant. She had tremendous presence. When she walked into the cantina, she owned it. Everyone at the bar turned to check her out. I could see them thinking, evaluating, wishing.

She looked to be in her mid-thirties. She wore a sweeping black skirt, an embroidered blouse, and a large silk scarf.

Malcolm whispered to me, "Trust fund baby. Lives for parties and social events. She's been writing a book for six years—a big bloody novel or some shit. Otherwise does nothing. But she knows everybody in Mexico."

She joined us at our table, turned her large black eyes to the side. The waiter appeared instantly at her side to take her drink order: Herradura and a glass of soda water with ice—extra limes.

Malcolm introduced us. She smiled, her lips tight and without a touch of lipstick. Then she lit a Faro cigarette and blew the smoke out the side of her mouth in order not to blow it in my face. She held the cigarette nicely between her fingers, head up, chin up, eyelids cast down like a lioness. Then she turned her eyes on me. "So what brings you to our tragic city?"

By *our*, it sounded more as if she meant hers. She had a mild British accent mixed with a hint of Spanish. Exotic.

"I'm looking for a woman," I said. I could tell she was someone you didn't waste time with. This was a chore for her. She was here as a favor to Malcolm.

"A biology student," I added quickly, "Maya Zavala."

Toni seemed to ponder this, her eyebrows furrowed just slightly. "Malcolm tells me she lived in La Roma?"

"That's what she put on her Facebook page," I said. "But the further I seem to get into it, the less truth I find."

She laughed. "Welcome to Mexico, my dear."

But it wasn't Mexico. I wasn't buying her magical realism bit. The craziness had started in Sarasota.

I showed her the photograph of Maya. I watched her eyes move slowly over the image. She pressed her lips together. Her lungs took in a long deep breath. Then she refocused on me. The intensity in her dark eyes vanished. "Yes. I know her."

It was as if someone had smacked me across the face. "You're kidding."

"Didn't I tell you?" Malcolm slapped me on the back and laughed like a drunken leprechaun. "Shit, Toni, you're fucking brilliant."

"Please, Malcolm, don't be vulgar." Toni set the photo down on the table. All our eyes fell on it. "She was Pricilla's roommate in that glorious old apartment on Plaza Luis Cabrera."

"Pricilla with the teeth?" Malcolm said. "What ever happened to that bird?"

Toni glared at him. "She went back to LA." Then she looked at me and in a snide tone added, "Couldn't handle La Ciudad."

"I liked her." Malcolm took a long sip of tequila. "She was all right."

"What about Maya?" I asked.

"I don't know," Toni said, but her tone had changed—concern. "She moved out. Found her own place, I suppose."

"So she stayed in Mexico?"

"I imagine," she said. "I didn't hear otherwise."

Malcolm glanced at me as if waiting for the next question, see what tricks I had under my sleeve. I leaned forward on the table. "Did she have any friends? Any places she liked to go to?"

"Maya?" She scoffed. "She was . . . funny."

Malcolm laughed.

She glared at Malcolm. "Not funny like that." She waved him off and turned her dark eyes on me. "She was a little odd. Independent. She abhorred groups. She went out when she wanted with whom she wanted. Yes, she was extremely independent. A rare quality in our expat community." She tilted her head to the side and glanced at Malcolm. "We tend to move in packs, like wolves. Don't we, Malcolm?"

"We're bloody disgusting," Malcolm said with a goofy smile. "Everyone sleeping with everyone else."

Toni raised her chin. "Yes. An incestuous bunch to say the least."

"But not her," I said.

"If I remember correctly, she was here to find some kind of reptile."

"The axolotl," I said.

She pointed at me with her cigarette. "Right. The axolotl. But there was something going on. She didn't want to join the folks at UNAM even though they'd been at it for months. And they had the funding. I remember Anita Solís did a piece on it: the search for the little axolotl. It was quite good, actually."

"I remember that," Malcolm said. "For the AP, right?"

Toni nodded. "That was in February, I believe. It got play in a lot of newspapers. She was quite proud. But Maya didn't want any part of that group. She wanted to do it all on her own."

"Do you reckon she was kidnapped?" Malcolm said. He wasn't laughing.

Toni shrugged. "Don't be so dramatic. Pricilla went back to LA. Maya must have found her own place. Mondragón said he saw her a few weeks ago at the gallery opening for that Cuban artist—"

"Fortuna," Malcolm said.

"He said she looked quite well."

"Her father hasn't heard form her in months," I said.

Toni raised an eyebrow. "Really? Is she a runaway?"

I leaned back and sighed. "Who knows what she is."

Toni smiled. "Knowing Maya she's probably out somewhere searching for the axolotl."

It was possible. Xochimilco was bigger than half of Sarasota. Maybe all of Sarasota. She could be anywhere.

"I'll put the word out," Toni said and took a generous sip of her tequila. She didn't even chase it with lime. "If she's around, I'm sure someone's seen her. No one just disappears from Mexico City. Not without one of us hearing about it."

* * *

I slept late the following morning. After breakfast I called Malcolm but got no answer. I took a taxi back to Xochimilco and found Ernesto hanging around the food stalls trying to hit up tourists to hire him as a guide.

"Dexter!" He seemed happy to see me. "Where we go today?"

"Back to the canals," I said.

"To find the students?"

"No," I said and looked around. It was past noon. There was a lot more activity than the previous morning. People were cooking, getting ready for the lunch crowd. A handful of tourists mingled around the water's edge, taking photos of the *trajinera* boats with their painted frames, cute names, and pretty flower arrangements.

"I just want to cruise around the canals again," I said.

"Why not take a *trajinera*? More fun."

"No. Is the old man around?"

"*Sí, claro.* Ausencio is always around." He led me past the road where two large tourist buses had just pulled up. We went back on the other side toward the water and found the old man leaning against the side of a food stall reading an adult comic book.

We loaded the little wooden boat with a plastic jug of gasoline and a couple of plastic bottles of drinking water and motored slowly into the narrower, more secluded waterways of Xochimilco.

We passed the Island of the Dolls. It didn't appear so creepy this time around. From the distance it looked like a bunch of trash. It reminded me of the debris after a tornado passed through a trailer park—all the twisted metal and insulation caught on the trees.

The day was hot and there was no shade. I was still a little hungover from the drinks. I leaned back and closed my eyes.

I had no plan. If Maya was trying to find the axolotl on her own, she had to be somewhere in the canals, working with her own team. The labyrinth of canals and lakes was complicated. It was impossible to search with any kind of order unless you had a team, like the folks from the UNAM. But I had no choice. So when Ernesto sat across from me and told me the old man wanted to know where to go, I said to tell him to get lost.

Ernesto laughed. "Lost, how?"

"Just cruise. Tell him to take me to the farthest place in Xochimilco. Where no one goes."

"You sure?"

I leaned back and let the sun fall on my face. "Yes, I'm sure."

We left behind the populated areas, the deformed *chinampas*, and went farther out where nature and farming covered the land. We occasionally saw a farmer hoeing his fields, walking between the rows of corn, children fishing, women hanging laundry. Except for the drone of the little engine and the stink of its exhaust, it was a perfect, peaceful afternoon.

The scenes—farmers with their hats and white shirts, toiling in the fields—reminded me of my grandfather's farm outside Gonzales, Texas. The place was a shit hole—a dozen acres and a handmade shanty with two cows, several goats, and a bunch of chickens. But when I was a kid, when we came to stay with him after my father died, it was paradise. His land seemed to spread out forever. It was as if he owned the world. And all I could think of back then was that I wanted to live there for the rest of my life.

He used to tell us stories of how difficult they'd had it back when he was a boy, working in the fields, traveling all year. But we were Americans now—brown-skinned, dark-eyed Americans. He was very clear about that, about being U.S. citizens, about speaking English, about being well educated, about having the same rights as everyone else. It wasn't that he didn't want us to be Mexican. He didn't want for us to suffer the prejudice and humiliation they had suffered. He didn't want us to break our backs working in the fields. He wanted better for us.

That's what got me into journalism in the first place. I wanted to contribute—to help. The world was shit. I had witnessed it in person when that cop shot my father. I wanted to fix things. But it was getting worse. In the end we'll all end up extinct like the goddamn axolotl.

I was surprised that we hadn't seen any boats or workers, biologists, students, or investigators all day. We'd been crusing along the canals for more than four hours and we'd seen absolutely nothing. When we passed the Island of the Dolls for the third time, I started to wonder if the old man was just going around in circles.

I told Ernesto to tell the old man to take us back. When we arrived in the main hub of Xochimilco, I invited Ernesto and the old man to a late lunch at one of the food stalls in the market. The old man and I drank cold Victoria beers and Ernesto—who insisted his parents said it was okay for him to drink beer, even though yesterday he told me he was an orphan—had an orange Fanta. We ate *gorditas* stuffed with chicken and *huaraches* with shredded pork and cheese, all of it cooked by hand and served with a smile by an old lady who kept staring at the old man, Ausencio.

When we finished, I explained to Ernesto my predicament. I had to find Maya. Our search was getting me nowhere, and I was running out of time. "I have to find her. But this, going around the canals by boat, is getting me nowhere."

He seemed to consider this very carefully, his head bowed, his hand on his chin—a real thinker. Then he bounced up and smiled. "Piojo. You must go to see el Piojo."

"Where's that?"

"Not where, who. He's a *brujo*. A doctor man. Witch doctor. He take care of many problems. He can help people see the future. He can help you find your friend."

"Right."

"No problem," he said. "I can take you. Is not far."

"Give me a break, Ernesto."

"*Esta bien, pues.* You tell me you don't know how to find this girl. I tell you to go see this man. You say no." He waved his finger at me. "You don't find your friend because you don't try."

"Get serious, Ernesto."

"This man Piojo, he very good. He give my sister abortion, no problem. No pain, no blood. He help my aunt with cancer. He told me one day I meet gringo, good gringo. We be best friends. And I meet you. Maybe he can find your friend."

"Yeah, and maybe not."

"*Claro.* Maybe not. But for three hundred and fifty pesos, is worth a try, no?"

I did the math—about twenty bucks.

"Unless, you don't want to try. Maybe in here." He tapped his chest. "You don't really want to find your friend."

"What the fuck does that mean?"

"My father always say, try every possible avenue."

"I thought you were an orphan?"

"I am."

Whatever. Ernesto was a little crazy, a con artist. Probably a glue sniffer. But he seemed to have a decent heart. He meant well. But I couldn't keep boating around the goddamn lakes and canals day in and day out. Besides, the fucking old man and his boat were not cheap. A *brujo*. Twenty bucks. What did I have to lose?

We took a taxi to Tláhuac and drove into a maze of small streets in a poor neighborhood that seemed to get poorer by the block. It was like diving into the bowels of a monster only to come out at the other end and drop on a dirty toilet that didn't flush. We went from paved streets to dirt streets—brown and dusty. None of the houses were painted. All the roofs had long stalks of rebar sticking out like antennas. The electric poles had dozens of narrow colored wires like a spiderweb. Everything looked homemade. And there was no traffic. No cars parked on the side of the street.

Finally, our taxi pulled over in front of a concrete block house with a Mexican flag waving at the end of the long pole that stuck out of the roof of the second floor. It was the tallest house in the neighborhood and the last one before the real slum spread out like a trash dump with small shacks built of wood scraps and cardboard.

Ernesto knocked on the large metal door. A small old woman led us into a small concrete patio where herbs and flowers grew out of cans and plastic buckets. On the wall there was an altar to the *Virgen de Guadalupe* with a few candles and wilting flowers that reminded me of my grandparents' living room.

We sat on plastic chairs and waited.

"What now?" I said.

"No problem." Ernesto made a gesture with his hand for me to chill.

I leaned back on the chair. The place smelled of soap and tortillas. A dog was barking somewhere in the neighborhood. I wondered about Maya—how she financed her life here. Mexico City wasn't cheap. The apartment, the search for the axolotl, food, transportation, it all had to add up to a pretty penny. The only thing I could figure was that the check Nick sent Maya for her rent at the hippie flophouse was somehow making its way back to her. Perhaps via Mike Boseman.

I pulled out my reporter's notebook and made a quick note: Maya's money. Someone had to be sending her money. But that still wouldn't help get Petrillo and Frey off my back. I had to find Maya. And when I did, I hoped she'd give me the name of someone with a motive to hurt her father.

After about fifteen minutes a large, heavyset man with long gray hair and a beard walked onto the patio and waved for us to come.

He led us into a room that resembled an office with a small metal desk, a few chairs, and a narrow military-style cot where it appeared someone had been sleeping. We sat across the desk from the *brujo*. No signs of witchcraft anywhere.

Ernesto spoke. The *brujo* nodded, his eyes moving from Ernesto to the wall, to me and back. I understood something about a woman, the axolotl and something about love. *Amor*.

I watched the *brujo's* hands, his chubby fingers fiddling over the desk, his fingernails long and dirty.

"*Sí*," the *brujo* said after a moment. "*Entiendo muy bien.*"

Ernesto smiled at me. "No problem. He fix everything."

The *brujo* walked slowly around the desk and pulled a few stones from his pocket and set them on the desk in front of him. Then he took out some herbs from the shelf behind him and some beads from a jar. He moved things around but said nothing. Then he sat and looked at Ernesto. "*Como se llama la mujer?*"

"Maya—" Ernesto turned to me. "What is last name of girl you like?"

"I don't like her. I'm just trying to find her."

"Okay. And the last name?"

"Zavala."

Ernesto glanced at the *brujo*. "Zavala."

The *brujo* nodded. He mumbled a few words to himself and moved the rocks and herbs around the desk. He wrote something on a piece of paper and raised his hand and chanted something. Then he looked down and seemed to meditate for a long time.

Ernesto bumped me on the side with his elbow and winked. Maybe something was happening for him, but it sure as hell wasn't happening for me.

After a moment the *brujo* raised his head and addressed Ernesto: "*Van a ser cuatrocientos pesos.*"

Ernesto turned to me. "It's four hundred pesos."

"You said three fifty."

He shrugged. "That was the price six months ago."

I counted out four hundred peso bills and gave them to Ernesto who gave them to the *brujo*. He folded the bills with great care and eased the money into his pocket. Then he motioned for me to follow him into another room.

This was more like it. There were dozens of candles and photos on a table in the corner of the room. On the other side was a set of shelves with plates and pots, arrangements with feathers and beads and two bowls burning with resin incense that smelled like a Catholic Mass.

He gestured for me to sit on a chair in the center of the room.

He walked circles around me, first quietly, then chanting in a language I didn't know. It certainly wasn't Spanish. He lit a cigar and blew smoke at me. He swept my arms and back with a bouquet of herbs and then tossed them on the floor at the foot of the table with the candles. There were no real dramatics, no skulls or smoking cauldrons. He just chanted and blew more smoke on me and then gave me two black river stones and three little beads to hold in my right hand. Then he led me to the table and motioned for me to place the stones and beads in a little pile next to an unlit candle.

He handed me a match and pointed to the candle. When I lit the candle, I noticed the small piece of paper where the *brujo* had written Maya's name. He had spelled her last name: San Bala.

CHAPTER TWELVE

THE FOLLOWING DAY I was lost. I had no idea what to do next. It didn't make any sense to return to Xochimilco. I would just be going around in circles wasting time and money. It was like looking for a needle in a field of haystacks. In retrospect, it would have been easier and less expensive to search for Tiffany back in Sarasota.

Still, I kept telling myself Maya was the better bet. She knew her father. She would know his friends, his enemies. Besides, Maya would have good reason to help me. Her father had been murdered. She'd want to find the killer. Get justice.

I told myself to be patient. Things would play themselves out. They always did. I had to wait and see what Toni might turn up.

I opened my Maya document and added a few notes and ideas. But I had nothing concrete. The big question that kept gnawing at the back of my head was money. If Nick had been sending Maya money, what was she going to do now? And who was going to inherit his fortune?

Later in the morning I left the hotel and walked across Reforma Avenue toward the center of town. There was no point in sitting around, waiting for the phone to ring.

Mexico City's quite the place, a blend of old and new, big city and small village. There was something very human about this city.

I ducked into Café La Habana on Bucareli Street for a bite to eat. The place was a throwback from the '50s. Even the waitresses and patrons looked as if they belonged in a different era. I sat by the large pane windows that faced the street and ordered enchiladas suizas and coffee.

I watched the people hustling up and down the street and tried to imagine Maya walking around here: her tall elegant figure, her thin arms swinging in the air, her high heels clicking against the pavement. From the photograph I had of her, she didn't seem like someone who would dive into the polluted waters of Xochimilco in search of a slimy amphibian. I couldn't see it. But what did I know? I couldn't just dismiss what Dr. Tabor at New College had said. He'd been very clear. Maya Zavala was ambitious.

I kept wondering about Nick. He never told me much about Maya. When it came down to it, I had very little information. I should have asked more questions. But then again, I didn't know he was going to be killed. That day at his house, it all seemed straightforward.

Almost too easy.

Why did Maya disconnect from her father? Maybe Nick was controlling, although he didn't come across that way to me. But who knew how people behaved with their own family. Maybe Maya was upset with him. Maybe she didn't like it that he let young girls like Tiffany into their home. What was up with that?

Nick had said Tiffany was a neighbor's daughter. Now that I had met her in person, I was pretty sure it was a lie. Tiffany didn't look or act like she came from a wealthy family. Not from a family that could afford a house in Sapphire Shores. And she didn't have the vocabulary of a college student. She was just plain, tough—like someone who'd been through some shit in her life. Maybe she was his dealer. Maybe that was the "stuff" she was after that day after Nick was killed.

Maybe.

I finished my meal and wandered. I was angry at myself for getting mixed up in all of this. It had been stupid and irresponsible. I knew nothing of what I was doing. I was a reporter not a detective. But it had been the money. The truth was that even if Nick had offered me a grand, I would have taken it.

I'd been seduced into this mess by Nick, by the money. But also by Maya. She was beautiful, mysterious. In the photograph she looked like the kind of person who would never give me the time of day, like a movie star, like someone who belonged in New York or Paris.

And yet there was something more. In a sense, Maya was no different from me. She was ambitious. She was making choices that the people close to her found selfish and egotistical: to become independent, to prove herself to her father, to search for the axolotl on her own, to make her own discovery, get the attention and praise. In many ways, Maya and I were cut from the same cloth.

I got lost in the back streets and emerged at a small park with a craft market. I wandered through the booths. I bought an embroidered dress for Zoe. But I didn't know her size. I was suddenly paralyzed in that little stall, staring at all the colorful dresses. The market lady showed me different items one after another, asking: "This one? How about this one?"

I knew nothing of my daughter. Did she even like flowers?

I ducked into another stall and paid a few good dollars for a fancy silver pendant from Taxco: a butterfly with turquoise and opal wings. Holly was going to love it.

Yes, Holly. She wouldn't leave my mind. I had to clear myself of this Nick and Maya business and try and get back together with her. She'd been the best thing for me when we were together. And the last few days had been wonderful. Could it be love?

Sure, why not?

* * *

When I finally walked into the lobby of the hotel, it was late afternoon. I checked in with the desk. Then I heard a woman's voice call my name: "Dexter Vega?"

It took me a moment to recognize Flor without the wet suit, the muddy face, the wet hair. She looked great in an embroidered cotton skirt like the one I'd bought for Zoe at the market and a black blouse. She wore her black shoulder-length hair combed neatly to the side.

"I've been waiting for you," she said. "Can we talk?"

"Of course." We went across the patio and sat on the chairs outside the bar. Julio brought us a couple of beers—Victorias because that was what Flor asked for.

"A couple of days ago, when you came to our field station, I couldn't talk honestly with you," Flor said, her eyes moving around the garden apologetically. "The students working with me are very protective of the axolotl and the work we are doing. They are very passionate about what this little animal means to us, to Mexico. They . . . I'm not sure how to put this . . . They do not want foreigners meddling with something they feel is uniquely Mexican."

"I can understand that," I said. "I hope I didn't rub anyone the wrong way. And if I did, please, I apologize."

"No, no." She smiled and touched my arm. "You were fine. It has nothing to do with you. But I didn't feel at liberty to discuss the woman you're searching for."

"Maya?"

She nodded and took a short sip of beer. "I couldn't talk to you about her in front of the students."

"You know her?"

"I'm the team leader for the search. I work directly with my professors at the university. I'm responsible for the work we do in the field. We spend all day together six days a week. We are a very tight group."

"Sure. I understand."

She leaned forward and stared at me. "I don't think you do."

"What do you mean?"

"When we were organizing the team at the start of the semester, I received an e-mail from Maya, the woman in your photograph. But her last name was not the one you mentioned, the Italian name—"

"Zavala?"

"Yes, it was Edwards. Maya Edwards."

"Are you sure it's the same person?"

She nodded. "She looked very much like the person in the photograph. And she was attending a college in Florida."

"New College?"

"Yes, I believe so. She had a very strong letter of recommendation from one of her professors—"

"Dr. Tabor."

"Yes, Dr. Albert Tabor. That was why my professor put her in contact with me. They wanted me to include her in the team."

"And she used the last name Edwards?"

She took a long drink of beer and leaned back on her chair and looked at me as if she were waiting for some comment or comeback from me. But I was dumbfounded. It wasn't adding up. Unless it was her mother's last name. Which was a strong possibility. Too many things were possible. What I didn't get was why Nick hadn't told me that. Also, if Dr. Tabor was her professor, he would have written the letter with her real name. And he never even mentioned Edwards. I was totally lost.

"So what happened?" I asked. I didn't know where to go with this.

"I did what my professors told me," she said. "I was not pleased with the arrangement. I had been promised autonomy to run the search. I'm the one who wrote the grant proposal. It is my grant. I wanted it to be my team."

"But the professors rule the class."

She smiled. "I'm only a graduate student. I accepted her, but I was reluctant. The others in the team were furious that a gringa was coming to help them find something that belonged to us."

"They didn't want her getting the credit."

"It always happens that way. If ten Mexicans are working on a project with one American, the American will get all the press."

"And the credit?"

She laughed. "Yes."

"So there's some serious backstabbing going on."

"We wanted to protect what is ours. And the team, they're young, idealistic. The axolotl—"

"I know, it's a symbol of national pride."

"It's more than that. For years we've had foreigners come here and explore, discover, extract. The axolotl is a very unique animal. There are thousands of them in captivity, but having a population in the wild is important because the breeding in captivity can alter the genetic makeup of the animal in the long term. We need them in the wild to keep them pure, the way they've been for centuries."

"I understand. And Maya was only interested in getting credit for the find so she could get into UC Davis or some other hotshot school."

Flor laughed, her hand over her mouth, her dark eyes squinting at me. "That was the same sense I had from her."

"So she worked with you?"

She shook her head, crossed her legs, and leaned forward, both arms on the table. "She came to Mexico, and I met her at the Librería Gandhi in Bellas Artes, downtown. We had a long and very productive conversation. She was well acquainted with the axolotl. But *she* wanted to work alone."

"And?"

"And nothing. I told her she had wasted her time and money. You can't do this kind of work alone. You can't dive into those canals without someone on the surface. And you need the maps and a detailed plan to work methodically one half acre at a time."

"She really thought she could do it?"

"I don't know what she was thinking. I only know my team of thirteen has been at it for eight months. We've covered over half the lakes and canals and we have found nothing."

I waved at Julio, gestured for another round. "Dr. Tabor told me she was very ambitious," I said.

"And stupid."

I was pissed and confused. Maya whatever-her-last-name was falling from grace pretty damn quick. But so was Nick. There was a lot of information he could have given me, but didn't. But I won't lie. I was curious as hell about Maya.

"You have any idea what might have happened to her?" I said.

Julio brought the beers. Flor wrapped her fingers around the neck of the bottle and laughed. "The cold beer is good after a day in the canals of Xochimilco."

"A cold beer is good anytime."

She smiled, tossed her head to the side. Her short black hair followed like a shiny wave. "Tell me, Dexter Vega, how do you fit into all this. Why are you looking for Maya?"

"Call me Dexter," I said. "And you didn't answer my question."

She had a sweet laugh. It was honest, from the gut. I liked that. "Dexter Vega. Are you Spanish?"

"My grandfather was from here."

"Really? You speak Spanish?"

"*Un poquito*," I said. "Enough to order beer, find the bathroom, and ask for help."

She laughed again. Probably getting a little buzzed, but I didn't mind. Not one bit.

"You know." She waved a finger at me. "I knew you had Mexican in you. I could tell."

"How's that?"

She shrugged. "I can just tell. I could see it in your eyes. In the way you moved."

"I'll take it as a compliment."

"You should."

I smiled and took a long sip of beer without taking my eyes off of her. She had not answered my question. But I didn't care. Fuck Maya Zavala or Edwards or whatever.

"We should get some dinner," she said, looking up at the red and black sky. In Mexico City there were no stars.

"Sure. They've got a restaurant—"

"*No, hombre*. I'll take you out. I'll show you a little hip corner of our city."

We took a taxi. The two of us in the backseat real close, her hand on my arm in a way that was friendly and then some. I leaned toward her.

We buzzed through the streets of the city. Traffic was light. The air was cool and surprisingly clean. After about twenty minutes, Flor leaned forward, her arm over the backrest of the front seat, and pointed to a street corner and said, "*Aquí*."

We stepped out of the taxi. She laced her arm around mine, and we walked the crowded sidewalk of the neighborhood called La Condesa. She said it was like the SoHo of the city. We ducked into a small bistro on the corner where we sat at a sidewalk table and where the waiter knew her by name.

She ordered the special for both of us. And more beer. Then she leaned over the table and locked her beautiful brown eyes with mine. "So, Dexter Vega. How do you like our city?"

"I like it a lot more now that I'm seeing it with you."

She smiled. She took compliments well. Not a bit shy.

Her eyes narrowed. "Can I ask you something?"

"Anything."

"What is the real reason you are so interested in finding Maya?"

I was surprised by the question. I had given her the lowdown in Xochimilco. Why didn't she believe it? "I told you. Her father hired me to find her."

"Yes, but why?"

"I don't—Because he hadn't heard from her in months. He was worried."

"You know he sent her money."

"I imagine he did."

"She was spoiled, but hated being that way."

The waiter brought the beers and an appetizer of escargots with a Bourguignonne sauce, which I had never tasted before. But what the hell.

"Why would she hate it?" I asked.

"I don't know. Pride. Or maybe she felt guilty. I think sometimes people who have it all don't know how to appreciate what they have."

We sucked down the appetizers.

"Be careful," she said and pointed at me with her fork. "They're a powerful aphrodisiac."

"What about you?" She had a great appetite. I leaned back on my chair and gave her my best sideways smile. "You never told me what happened to her."

She frowned. "I didn't?"

I nodded.

She looked down at her plate. "She went at it on her own."

"What, looking for the salamander?"

"It's not a salamander."

"Sorry. You know what I mean."

"Please," she said, "treat it with respect. It deserves at least that, no?"

The waiter brought the food. Huachinango Veracruz style. Mighty tasty red snapper.

"I saw her a couple of times in Xochimilco. Once she passed by our location on a launch. She looked at us but didn't wave or acknowledge us. Just moved on, looking at us like we were cattle feeding on the side of the canal."

"And then?"

She pointed at me with her fork. "You are a very impatient man, Dexter Vega."

"Jesus, Flor. Can you call me Dexter?"

"No. I like Dexter Vega. Dexter is too small, too gringo."

I laughed. "Okay, go on."

"I saw her again about three months ago at the food market in Xochimilco. She was sitting alone at a table eating tacos. She didn't see me, and I didn't approach her."

"And that's it?"

She raised her hands. "*Eso es todo.*"

We had dessert and a shot of cognac and then walked together, her arm laced with mine, her body leaning slightly against me. It was easy to be with her, here, surrounded by all the hipness of the city. The sidewalk and restaurants were busy, crowded with wealthy Mexicans. We came up to a four-story art deco building. Flor pointed up. "This is me."

"Home?"

She nodded and looked away with a tight little smile. "Would you like to come up?"

She lived in a small apartment on the third floor. It was decorated in a way that reminded me of a classy Mexican restaurant, but with personality. She set her bag down, served a couple of tequilas, and we had a toast.

"To you," I said.

"To Maya, for bringing you here."

We sipped the nectar of the Aztec Gods. We moved closer, her eyes on mine like a hawk. I set my glass down and took her in my arms. The rest is history.

*　*　*

When I woke up in the morning, Flor was gone. She had left a note on the door: *Make yourself at home. Coffee on the stove. Went to find the axolotl.*

CHAPTER THIRTEEN

WHEN I GOT back to my hotel, the desk clerk handed me a note: *Meet me at the end of the lake in Chapultepec Park where the children learn to bullfight. M.*

I laughed. Nice. Malcolm was full of drama and mystery, but he couldn't keep a fucking appointment. For a moment I contemplated not going. But then I thought of Toni. Maybe Malcolm had gotten word from her.

I tried calling Malcolm, but he didn't answer. I didn't leave a voice mail. I went up to my room and did some Googling. I found Maya Edwards. She was a student registered at New College. She had a closed Facebook page. I sent her a friend request just for the hell of it. She was also mentioned in a couple of news articles—one was in the *Sarasota Herald* about New College students making the grade beyond the classroom. The other was her mother's obituary in the *Naples Daily News*. It said she died in 2006 and was survived by her only daughter, Maya. There was no mention of Nick Zavala.

Then I looked up Flor Quintero in Mexico. I sent her a friend request on Facebook and looked over some of her articles on the axolotl, but they were all in Spanish. From what I could make out, she'd been studying the little critter for seven years. A census in 2003 counted nearly a thousand axolotl. A decade later, in 2013, it counted zero.

I knew nothing of this little animal, but it struck me to know that in just ten years they had been wiped out from that giant lake.

I empathized with Flor. And Maya. Damn. I guess I was getting attached to the damn water lizard.

I made some more notes on my Maya document. Now, the big gaping hole was why did Nick not tell me she was going by her mother's last name? What was the connection here? If Nick was her father by way of Maya's mother, wouldn't he be mentioned in the obituary? Just as things began to come together, they broke up again. Nothing seemed to line up.

I took a quick shower and grabbed a taxi to Chapultepec Park—Mexico City's version of Central Park—a huge green expanse with a zoo and a lake and an old castle atop a hill that had been turned into a museum. I walked along a trail and found an old man selling ice cream from a little cart. I tried my best Spanish on him, inquiring about the place where the children learned to bullfight. He tilted his cowboy hat and pointed toward the lake. "*A la orilla del lago*," he said, something about the side of the lake.

I bought a scoop of mango ice cream on a cone from the old man and walked along the bend of the lake. In a small clearing in the distance, a man was working with half a dozen little boys. He yelled directions at them. One of the boys held a pair of bullhorns on his head and charged at another boy holding a red bullfighting cape. The other boys watched in silence. The place where children learn to bullfight.

But Malcolm wasn't around. Nobody was. I tried calling him on my cell phone, but it went directly to voice mail. I looked out at the lake, green and opaque like the canals of Xochimilco. I wondered if there was any life in there. Maybe frogs. I turned back to face the park. One of the boys had broken away from the group of young bullfighters and was running to where I was. When he caught up with me, he stopped and bowed. Then he extended his hand, offering me a folded piece of paper. "Señor Vega?"

I took the paper, and he ran back to the bullfighting lesson. I read the note: *I'm behind the castle.*

I put the note in my pocket and glanced up at the big castle in the distance. What the fuck? I started walking, slowly, looking at the young couples in rowboats on the lake, eating my ice cream, listening to the whistle of the man selling balloons.

I came around the side of the hill. There was no one around, except two men in suits and sunglasses about thirty, forty yards away. I glanced up at the castle. Maybe he'd meant up in the castle. I tossed what was left of my ice cream cone in a trash bin and pulled out my phone to call Malcolm.

"Why are you looking for me?" A woman's voice, deep, confident.

I turned around. Maya. She wore denim jeans, leather boots, and a burgundy coat. She was stunning. Her eyes were like water—not just the color, they were liquid. Her entire person seemed to glow like the sun. And yet, she looked sad.

I swallowed hard, my saliva thick with the taste of mango. "Your father," I managed to blurt out like a starstruck teenager. "He's dead." It just came out of me like vomit. I'd been caught off guard. I had been expecting Malcolm's ugly mug, his hunched shoulders, a stinky Faro cigarette protruding form his fat lips. But this—

"I know," she said. "He died when I was a little girl."

I gestured with my hands, reaching out, then hung them on the sides of my waist. "I don't think you understand. Nick's been murdered."

Her face was like ice. "Nick Zavala is not my father."

"Look, I don't know what's going on here. But Nick's dead, and the cops are looking at me as their prime suspect."

"And, did you?" We were eight, maybe ten, feet from each other. She kept her hands in the side pockets of her jacket.

"What, kill Nick? No. Jesus. He asked me to find you—"

"Are you a detective?"

I laughed and shook my head. "My name's Dexter Vega. I'm . . . I'm an unemployed journalist."

She turned her head slightly and looked in the direction of the two men in suits. There was something about her manner, her movements, her voice. She was calm, royal. Like how a princess might behave.

"That man," she said with a narrow grin, "he never gave up."

"What man? Nick? What's going on?" I was feeling smaller and smaller, but I was also getting a little angry.

"You say you're a reporter?"

"Was."

"Your career ended with a job?"

I hadn't thought of it that way. Here I was by Chapultepec Park and I didn't know if I was a reporter, a detective. And who the hell was this woman?

"Do you mind if we walk?" she said, and we started off back toward the front of the castle. She smelled of expensive perfume, sweet.

"I was running away from Nick," she said suddenly. "I didn't want to be found. I learned of his death from an acquaintance in Sarasota. Then I heard you were in Mexico City looking for me." She paused for a moment and glanced at me. "Why did Nick want you to find me?"

"I don't know. He said you were his daughter and that you were missing. He paid me a lot of money."

"And that made sense to you?"

"Why wouldn't it?"

"Do you have any children, Mr. Vega?"

"I have a daughter. Zoe. And please, call me Dexter."

She smiled and looked at the path ahead. Around the side of the lake we could see people making their way toward the entrance to the castle. "I don't how to describe Nick. Who he was. What he was."

She sounded angry—subdued venom.

"My real father died when I was two. He was not a great man. I suppose you'd say he was average. But like most people, he didn't expect to die so young. There was no insurance. Just debt."

"I'm sorry."

She laughed in a way that was supposed to make me feel at ease but kind of spooked me. She had total control of herself.

"My mother dated a man who became a problem for me so I ran away from home. I was fourteen. I lived in the streets for a few months. Then I met Nick. He took me in. You could say he took care of me. But he wasn't my father."

"I'm sorry. I didn't know. Nick was worried about you. He hadn't heard from you—"

"Nick didn't hear from me because I didn't want him to hear from me. I didn't want to be with him. I wanted out of his world."

I stopped walking and looked at her, tall, beautiful. The sunlight filtered through the trees and spilled around us in little spots. "I'm not getting it."

She smiled.

"His world?"

She looked at the ground and began to walk. "How well did you know Nick, Mr. Vega?"

"Not very well," I said. "We actually met at a bar and he offered me the job of finding you. It seemed simple enough at the time."

"Nick Zavala was a very sick man. He picked up girls from the streets, young teenagers, twelve, thirteen, maybe older. Fourteen in my case, and forced us to have sex with him."

For a moment, all I could hear were children's voices, calling out names, saying, "*Aqui, aqui.*" Across from us, a small group of boys in school uniforms were playing soccer. And in my blurred vision

I saw my daughter, Zoe. Something inside me was emptying out, a silence, confusion. I was struck with a sharp wave of nausea. It was as if the ground was sucking down my feet, my legs.

Maya nodded. "He took us in, cleaned us up, took care of us, fed us well, gave us alcohol and drugs. But we had to pay him back with our bodies. When you're fourteen, fifteen, there is a part of it that feels like you've won the lottery: a fancy house with a pool, drugs, food, friends. A perpetual party. You don't see it because you're still a kid. You're blind to the sickness. It's a thousand times better than being in the streets or a shelter. I mean, he was rich. You could almost say we had a nice life there."

"And then?"

"And then you get it. You understand what's going on. How this man is abusing your body. Violating you. You can't say no to him when he comes in your room. You want to escape, but you can't."

"I'm sorry. I—"

"It wasn't that we were prisoners. But we had nowhere to go. There comes a point where sex just becomes this abstract thing. You turn off, I suppose. You want to leave but you don't want to leave."

"I didn't know."

She looked away for a moment. "He didn't hold anyone against their will. Not by force. Except me."

"Why?"

She shrugged. "Nick didn't know how to let go of me. He could let go of everyone else. Girls were always coming and going from his place. But me? He wanted me there." Maya stopped walking again. She ran her hand through her hair and looked at me. "He was obsessed with me. He paid for my school, sent me to New College. I was everything to him: daughter, wife, lover. But I just wanted out. I hated him."

"So you came up with this axolotl project to get you out of town."

She was looking away at the lake. A pleasant wind was blowing and her hair was gliding like a dream. Her presence was like a treasure, like being at a museum. There was something incredibly powerful about her. She spoke so freely of this, of Nick's perversions.

"I thought he would forget about me. That time away from me would ease his hunger for me. But it did the opposite. He sent me a check every month." She looked at me. "He had other girls. That was never an issue. He had them young, willing and unwilling. He had everything he wanted. But he wanted to possess me completely, and that was something he couldn't have. I think that with people like Nick, it's about absolute power. He wanted what he couldn't have. Maybe that was part of his sickness. Maybe he wanted children because they were forbidden."

"Jesus . . ." I put my hands to my face, massaged my cheeks, my forehead, my temples. My mind swirled with thoughts of Nick, Tiffany, Maya. And Zoe.

The cops knew nothing about this. Or if they did, they didn't let on. I felt queasy. I took a deep breath and stepped back. "I'm sorry," I said, and shook my head violently like I was trying to exorcise a demon. "I didn't know. I didn't know him."

She placed her hand on my shoulder and moved her head close to mine. "Don't be a victim, Mr. Vega. Don't put it on you. Don't let him win. The things he did, with me and the others, we—"

She stopped abruptly. I looked at her. I felt like a child in her presence. All my problems became tiny.

"Nick was a manipulator," she said.

"But you were children," I said. "You were high on drugs. You had no control."

She smiled and pressed my shoulder. "No. We were grown up. We were twelve, fourteen, sixteen, but we had grown up. If it hadn't been Nick who picked us up and, I suppose in a way saved us, it

would have been some pimp working off the North Trail. Some of
the girls that left never found anything better. From there, it only
got worse for most of them. Sexual abuse turns your brain inside
out. It kills your soul. You don't know how to function in real life.
And the streets . . . you don't know how it is. For those of us who
ended up with Nick . . . you could say we were lucky."

It didn't sound that way to me. And it was wrong. I felt cheated.
Tricked. I could only imagine how she and the others felt. If Nick
weren't dead, I would kill him. What did he fucking expect from
me?

But then I knew. If he hadn't been killed, I would have told him
Maya was in Mexico City and he would have come to get her back.
Or maybe not. Ten thousand fucking dollars.

I hated myself. I would have done it. I was a whore. "So what
now?" I asked.

"I want you to forget about me."

"Why?"

"I want to disappear, Mr. Vega. I'm happy here. I'm making a life.
A new life with new friends and no past. Nick doesn't exist here."

"What about the axolotl?"

She smiled the way a friend smiles when you talk about a pleasant memory. "I will forever be grateful for the axolotl. And for
Dr. Tabor who pointed out their existence to me. They helped me
escape."

"So you don't care about the axolotl?"

"I care a great deal. I care about all living beings. But I'm not investigating their existence. No."

I laughed. "Tabor said you were terribly ambitious."

"Not ambitious, Mr. Vega. Desperate. The axolotl was my only
way out of hell."

"Why didn't you go to the cops?"

She laughed and looked away. "It's complicated. When you're picked up from the street like a piece of trash and then given all these luxuries and the years pass, at some point you start feeling as if it was your doing, that you wanted it, that it's your fault that these things happened to you—that you were not held hostage but were a guest. Believe me, it's a lot to deal with. The guilt over what I've lived through in the last ten years will never disappear."

We walked a little farther, leaving the castle behind and walking toward the lake. I wasn't sure whether she was leading the way. Maybe I was. I was afraid to ask about Nick, about her life. I kept thinking of Tiffany, too. How many more were there?

"It's complicated," she said suddenly. "When you're in it, in that world, it feels normal."

She grabbed my arm, her fingernails digging hard against my skin. "Somewhere in the back of my head I knew it was wrong. But I was powerless. I didn't know how to do it. Like kicking a habit you don't know you have."

She was shaking. I embraced her, my arm around her shoulder, and she pressed her face against my chest and allowed a single soft sob to escape her lips.

"I'm so sorry," I said.

She stepped back and shook her head. "Don't," she said. "Don't feel sorry for me. I don't want you or anyone's sympathy or help. I just want to disappear and live a normal life."

"I understand."

She backed away from me and wiped her tears with a handkerchief. Then she smiled. "Thank you."

We started walking again, my hand touching her elbow. I thought of her situation, how someone like Nick was allowed to exist. How I had been roped into this when all I ever wanted was to be a journalist, to break these stories, to help people who did not have a voice, or did not have the foresight to see the wrong that was being done to them. But instead I was being used. I had been used by the newspaper and I had been used by Nick.

If my father's murder at the hands of a policeman and my years as a journalist had not turned me sour on humanity, this did. I was that much closer to becoming a cynic, of never believing in this shitty world of sick, opportunistic fucks. It was as if the things that made us human had vanished from our genes, washed out like Flor had said about the axolotl in captivity. We were no longer humans. Humanity was extinct like the axolotl. Gone from our hearts was the most important trait we had once possessed: trust.

Except I could see some of that in Maya. Despite everything she had lived through, she had dug her way out. She smiled and managed herself in a way that offered hope. Whether she cried herself to sleep or had nightmares was something only she would know.

She stopped walking and turned to face me. "So, we're good?"

I nodded.

"I hope I was able to help you."

"You did."

She took a short step back and bit her lower lip.

"Just one thing," I said. "Do you have any idea who might have killed him?"

She turned her eyes to me. "It could have been anybody. He was involved in drugs. He could have crossed a pimp. Picked up the wrong girl."

I nodded, but she was walking away, back toward the castle.

"Maya," I said. "How did you know I was looking for you?"

She paused. Then she turned slightly and looked at me, her hair covering her sad liquid eyes. "An axolotl told me."

* * *

Back at my hotel I opened the Maya document and entered all the information, every detail, every nuance. The parts were adding up, but the story was as fractured as ever. I had found Maya, but all it had done was open a whole other chapter in this nightmare. Nick Zavala was a disease that kept spreading. It didn't put me any closer to the murderer. If anything, it made me feel like a bigger fool than ever. I had been duped and bribed with ten grand to do the bidding of a pig—to find the victim of a pedophile.

Unless Maya was lying.

Sexual abusers did not have consistent profiles—that's what made them so dangerous. They were different. It made sense about Nick: the sex toys, the drugs, his obsession for Maya. And Tiffany. She couldn't be more than seventeen—probably younger. And she certainly looked like a runaway when I met her outside Zavala's house.

Everything I looked over in my notes, everything I corrected, everything I tried to connect fell apart about halfway to nowhere. I was going to have to go back to Sarasota and face the cops. Even if I could show them that Nick had been abusing young girls, it didn't guarantee I would come off their radar. Murder was still murder. There was still a 50/50 chance I could be indicted. They just had to come up with a motive, and that crackerjack team had done it before. They could do it again. There was no such thing as throwing oneself at the mercy of the law. I had written too many stories on how the Sarasota PD shot first and asked questions later. There were too many homeless men and unarmed black men that had been physically abused and even shot to death by Sarasota's finest. And nothing ever came of it, not even temporary suspension for the officers involved. If they wanted to pin this on me, they would. And the way Petrillo and Frey had acted the last time I'd met them made me feel they were desperate to hang Nick's murder on someone. I was the closest thing they had to guilty.

CHAPTER FOURTEEN

I SHOULD HAVE packed up my things and taken the next flight out. That would have been the logical thing to do. Get the fuck out of Mexico. Go face the music. Maybe even walk into the DA's office with Brian Farinas and offer them my help, give them a full confession.

I had found Maya, and while she'd shed an ugly light on Nick Zavala, it did not get me any closer to the murderer. My sights were now on Tiffany. I'd had two options and I'd chosen the wrong one. Now that Maya had shown me who Nick was, I realized the answer to who murdered Nick probably lay with Tiffany.

I'd fucked up.

And now I was doing it again. All my evidence, my crazy Maya document, and even what little intuition I had about this kind of thing, was telling me to go back, come clean with the cops, and move on with my life. But instead of leaving and going home to Sarasota, I stayed.

Flor awoke something in me that had been lost in limbo ever since I was laid off from the damn paper. That one night with her was like a breath of fresh air. Being with her reminded me why I was put on this earth in the first place. Seeing her enthusiasm for the axolotl, her perseverance and belief in its importance for Mexico and the human race had led her on a seven-year investigation and an eight-month search in the mud of Xochimilco. Despite finding nothing, she hadn't stopped searching. And she was not going to stop until she found it.

And I suppose in a way, she had hope for me. Maybe she didn't realize it but she had given me hope in myself.

I was convinced I should go home and face the music, settle the business of Nick's murder with the cops and expose the man for what he really was, find Tiffany—who could lead me to the murderer—and be done with this business. But I couldn't go. Not yet.

I wanted to be here, in this city of stone and smoke. I wanted to lie next to Flor, caress her hair and feel her heart beating against my flesh. She was like a tonic. She made me feel alive. I wanted more of that. I wanted all I could get from her. And I wanted to offer her whatever she needed—encouragement, admiration for what she was doing—for what she gave me. So I did what every fool who is falling for a woman would do: I invited her to dinner.

We met at nice little restaurant in La Roma, the neighborhood where Maya once lived. It looked like an extension of La Condesa, the hip neighborhood where Flor lived. But La Roma felt more open, more residential in some sections. The place she chose, El Traspatio, was a funky outdoor place with a lot of wood and stone in the yard of a large house. It was quaint and hip, and housed in a tiny space that brought us closer together. It was perfect.

We ordered a bottle of Rioja and arrachera steak and grilled vegetables. The waiter poured the wine and we had a toast to the axolotl. Flor took my hands and held them and gave me a sly smile. "Speaking of which, did you find *your* axolotl?"

"You did that?"

She shook her head.

"You told Maya to meet me at the park?"

She shook her head again and hid her smile behind our hands. "I know what it's like to search for something and not find it."

"So you did."

"No," she said. "I only wish I knew how it feels to find what you've been looking for for a long time."

I squeezed her hands. I was sure it had been her. She must have set it up. This whole time I'd been thinking Toni had gotten in touch with her. One thing I was sure of: it couldn't have been the *brujo*. I didn't believe in him, and he'd spelled her name wrong.

"I can tell you this," I said. "When you find what you've been searching for, you'll be surprised at what you actually find."

"In a good way, I hope."

"I don't think it's good or bad. It just . . . is."

"When I find my axolotl, I know exactly what will happen. I will be the happiest woman in Mexico. And I will have the evidence to change how we manage our patrimony."

I laughed. "You're an activist."

"We're all activists," she said. "But here, in Mexico, it's a very tough battle. Everything's corrupt. You move one step forward, and they push you back two."

The waiter brought our steaks—grilled over charcoal in the corner of the yard—medium, glistening with juice and a dab of chimichurri. Delicious.

After dinner we took a long walk down Alvaro Obregon, a wide avenue with a pleasant canopy, crossed Avenida Insurgentes, and wandered into La Condesa and back up to Flor's apartment.

After we'd made love, she rested her head on my chest and hummed a song I'd never heard before. I was so relaxed, I wanted to stay that way forever. This was what had been missing from my life for too many years. I was far away—a vacation from my obsessive mind, from my problems, from Maya and Nick and the Sarasota PD—and from my ridiculous dead career. But as much as I wanted the moment to never end, I had to face reality. Worse, I had to tell Flor.

"I have to leave in a couple of days," I said without looking at her.

She didn't seem to flinch or tense a single muscle. Her foot tangled with mine at the end of the bed. Her hand moved gently over my chest.

"Flor . . ."

"I know, Dexter."

"I wish I didn't."

"What I wonder," she said, "is whether you'll come back."

"Of course I will. You have to show me the rest of the city."

She laughed.

"I'm sorry," I said. "If I didn't have this mess hanging over—"

She put her hand over my lips. "Stop worrying about the unavoidable. You have to let go of the things you cannot control. Sometimes you have to allow fate to do its job. Relax. Enjoy the moment."

I closed my eyes, but all I could see was Holly. It was as if she were there, looking down at me with a mischievous grin I couldn't interpret. Guilt poked at me from all angles. This was wrong. What the fuck was I doing here?

When I opened my eyes again, it was morning and Flor had already left for Xochimilco in her quest for the axolotl.

* * *

I spent the morning wandering through La Condesa. I was in no hurry to go anywhere, much less go home to Sarasota to face whatever was waiting for me there. I ended up in Chapultepec Park and then crossed Reforma Avenue. I checked out the Rufino Tamayo Museum of Art and had lunch at a hole in the wall on Calle Victor Hugo.

Afterwards I went into the Hotel Camino Real to exchange some money and find a taxi. I considered having a drink at the bar. A cold beer or tequila—a good quality reposado. It was a nice modern bar with a lot of light. A good place to sit and think. But I dismissed the idea. I wanted to stay sober. I made my way up the long steps in the lobby and noticed a man in a gray suit who seemed vaguely familiar. He leaned forward with his head bowed, reading something inside a folder. My instinct was that it was someone famous—a movie star. As I came closer along his right side, I saw the outline of his face. He had long blond hair and a nice tan.

"Mike?"

He glanced up and slapped the folder shut.

"Mike Boseman?"

The color drained from his complexion. Literally. Surprise and confusion all over him. He shoved the folder under his arm and stared at me, his eyes wide.

"I'm sorry, do I know you?" His words stumbled out from under his tongue. It was a far cry from the way he'd greeted me at his house. Where was the confidence, the bravado, the attitude?

"Sarasota. Siesta Key, actually." I put my hand out. "Dexter Vega."

He looked at my hand before shaking it. "I'm sorry," he said. "I'm not making a connection."

He was clean-shaven, hair neatly combed to the side like a good executive. He looked the furthest thing from the scruffy rich surfer who yelled at me from the second-story window of his Gulf-front mansion.

"I was outside your house in Point of Rocks last week. I was looking for Maya Zavala."

"Oh, right." His eyes darted across the lobby, left and right. When they landed back on me, he asked, "What are you doing in Mexico City?"

"Looking for Maya. And you?"

He looked down, at his shoes, back at me. "Business."

"How long are you here for?"

He spat out a fake, nervous laugh. "Not really sure." He paused, and for a moment he seemed at a loss for words. "You know how it is," he added quickly. "Everything here's *mañana, mañana, mañana.*"

I laughed, trying to put him at ease. I had so many questions for him, but I didn't want to spook him because he looked like a chicken ready to fly the coop.

"You're not getting back in the movie business, are you?"

"No, no. I'm done with that. Learned my lesson the hard way, right?"

"New venture? Need a partner? Investors?" Now I was the one who laughed nervously. This was too much of a coincidence. I was sure he was here for the same reason I was.

"Well, it's still early for that," he said. "We're only in the planning stages."

I didn't want to lose him. "You staying here?"

He looked around as if trying to recognize where he was. Then he shook his head. "No, no. I'm staying up in . . . in, hum. At a friend's place in Polanco."

"That's great." I was right back on him. "Lucky you. You get to experience the real Mexico."

"Yeah," he said and took a step to the side. People were walking up and down the steps. "I suppose I will."

"So I stopped by your house before coming here. It was all shuttered up. I thought you'd gone up north for the summer."

He nodded, smiled. Sweat was building in tiny drops on his forehead. I needed answers.

"Nah, just here," he said. "But from here I have to go to California."

"Surfing?"

"What?"

"In California. You surf, right?"

He forced a chuckle. "Maybe. But business before pleasure."

He was lying. I was sure of that. One hundred percent. "So where you headed now?"

"Yeah . . . I have some appointments I need to . . ."

"Sure. I know how it is. Business. I'll walk you out. You're getting a taxi?"

"No, no. It's fine. I'm fine."

We walked to the exit. He was slipping from my grip. But I couldn't let him go. Finally I spat it out: "Any news from Maya?"

"Maya? No, nothing."

"She's here, though. Right?"

"I . . . I suppose."

"So you don't know where she is?"

He shook his head. "No. I suppose she's working, looking for the water lizard."

"The axolotl."

"Right."

"You think you'll see her while you're here?"

"I don't know," he said and looked past me. We were outside the front door. Taxis were parked along the driveway, bellhops were loading and unloading luggage. The doorman approached us, asked if we needed a taxi.

"But you guys are still dating, right?"

Boseman ignored my question and spoke to the doorman. "Yes, taxi." Then he smiled at me. "Well, I'll see you around . . ."

"Dexter," I reminded him. "Dexter Vega. The guy who's looking for Maya." A large black taxi pulled up. The doorman was right on it. He opened the back door and smiled.

"Right." Boseman nodded and slipped into the car. "Look me up when you're back in the old SRQ. We'll have a drink or something. Share Mexico stories."

* * *

Just as the case was finally coming together, it collapsed. Back to square one. Or maybe not. Boseman could be in Mexico with Maya—or he could be here looking for her. He could be bringing her money. Whatever the reason, I was certain he was here because of her. I hadn't nailed him the way I'd wanted to but it was obvious that seeing me had freaked the shit out of him. Something was fishy. But what bothered me the most was that I had just settled everything with Maya. As far as I was concerned the case of Maya Zavala—Edwards—was closed. Now Boseman showed up and fucked it all up. But why?

He came to join her. No, that was too perfect.

I stood outside the Camino Real trying figure it out. Then I realized one thing: seeing Boseman gave me an excuse to stay in Mexico a few extra days. I could postpone my exit. I could see Flor. A few more days in old Mexico would be grand.

I rushed back to my hotel and updated my Maya document. But as I looked over my notes, I realized the case was not quite closed. It couldn't be. Maya gave me the skinny on her father. Mike Boseman was here to join her. But I didn't like it. Call it intuition. Rich fucks like him rub me the wrong way. Suddenly it was all right there in front of me: Maya. She had a pretty strong motive. Maybe she planned this whole thing with Boseman. The two of them would get the inheritance and disappear.

Shit.

I closed my computer. Then my phone rang. It was Malcolm. He wanted me to attend a party tonight in the Palmas neighborhood at the home of the correspondent for the *New York Times*.

CHAPTER FIFTEEN

THE PARTY WAS at a large swanky house in a wealthy neighborhood in the hills. It didn't even feel like we were in Mexico. They had waiters and a caterer and a bartender and a trio playing top forties with a jazzy feel—food, booze, and even an ice sculpture.

"If you're a journalist in Mexico, you have to attend these parties," Malcolm said. He had two whiskeys, one in each hand. "It's one of the perks of the profession. You meet your colleagues, maybe make some decent contacts, and get loaded on free booze."

My mind was buzzing. I was impressed and pissed. My newspaper was laying off reporters while the *New York Times* correspondents were living high on the hog: the house, living expenses, maids, cars, and a monthly trip out of Mexico City so they could get out of the smog—all courtesy of the company.

"Check it out." Malcolm raised one of his glasses and gestured at the crowd. There had to be sixty, seventy people. "The Mexican businessmen and politicians always hang out together. I'm sure they're making deals, figuring out how to get richer. As if any of 'em needed more bloody money."

He pointed at a small group standing together on the patio. "And that little group over there, those are the staff correspondents talking over each other about their latest scoops. And over on that side is the Mexican press and some of our resident freelance photographers."

I glanced at Malcolm. He was swaying back and forward, buzzing with drink. "And where do you fit in?" I said.

"I don't." He laughed. "I'm a free agent, ey?"

I grabbed a beer and watched the crowd, but my mind was spinning, trying to figure out what was going on with Maya and Boseman. What the hell was he doing in Mexico?

I ran it all through my head: the hippies said Maya lived with Boseman on the beach. Then Maya left for Mexico to look for the axolotl, but that was just a front to get away from her father. When Nick lost contact with Maya he hired me because I was a dumb-ass.

It was possible Maya planned this whole thing with Boseman. It was possible they planned Nick's murder. It very well could have been Boseman. Or maybe Boseman was acting alone. Maybe he found that Nick had been abusing Maya. Love is a great motivator. I could see Boseman doing it as a favor to Maya—a revenge killing. Or they could have done it for money. Greed, another great motivator.

That's what kept poking at my gut: money. I had to find out who was getting the loot: the house, the art collection, the cash. Boseman might be well off, but he wasn't rich like Nick Zavala. Besides, I had the feeling someone of Boseman's character could never have enough money. I should have asked Maya about Boseman, whether he knew what Nick had been up to. Damn. I had so many questions.

Malcolm nudged me. "Look there."

Toni Spencer had just walked in. She looked amazing, elegant. She was accompanied by a thin Mexican man with a long gray ponytail.

"Aurelio Hernández," Malcolm said. "They say he's the next big thing in the art world. Protégé of Francisco Toledo."

Everyone in the room looked their way. There was a buzz. A handful of guests made their way to them.

"What do you say we have a couple more drinks," Malcolm said, and placed his empty on a side table. "Then go downtown. There're

some freaky strip joints with live sex acts in Garibaldi. You ever experience a Mexican table dance?"

"I'm not here on vacation."

"So? Take a break. Have a little fun."

"I can't. Not just yet."

"I thought you said you found the bird you were looking for."

I shook my head. How he managed to write articles for major
international publications was beyond me.

"I need to talk to Toni," I said.

"Good luck."

I grabbed a beer and made my way through the crowd to the
front of the living room. I snuck up from the side and tapped Toni's
arm. "Remember me?"

She smiled. Her gesture seemed exaggerated, as if she was really
glad to see me. "But of course. Dexter, my dear. Any news?"

"Of Maya?"

"Wasn't that who you were looking for?"

I smiled. One of the Mexican reporters was raising his voice, barking questions at Aurelio Hernández who was cowering behind Toni.

Toni grabbed his arm. "*Déjalo en paz, no? Dale chance de disfru-
tar la fiesta.*"

The man backed away. Toni rolled her eyes and laced her arm
around mine. "Aurelio is putting together a very politically charged
exhibit. There's a rumor going around that the PRI, Mexico's ruling
political party, is funding the whole thing."

I nodded.

"You have no idea what I'm talking about, do you?"

"I just got here a few days ago."

She laughed. "How refreshing."

We walked together to the side of the living room near where the
band had just stopped playing.

"I asked around for Maya." She looked genuinely concerned. "But no one appears to have seen her in weeks. I don't know what I can tell you. If it's Narcos, she's probably doomed. She could be dead. Have you considered contacting the embassy?"

"I saw her," I said.

Her eyes widened. "You did?"

"Yes, at the park. We spoke. Briefly."

"Is she all right?"

"Seems to be. She's doing her thing. She didn't want her family to chase after her. It's all taken care of."

"I'm glad to hear that." She waved at someone behind me. "Will you be staying long?"

"Maybe a couple more days."

"You should come for dinner. I'm having a few people over on Wednesday."

"Thanks, but I don't think I'll be staying that long."

"Either way." She moved to the side and gave me a kiss on the cheek. "I like you, Dexter. Don't be a stranger."

I grabbed her arm. "Thank you, Toni."

"I didn't do a thing."

"But you did." I wasn't sure if it had been she who set up my meeting with Maya. But just in case, I threw the question out there: "Any chance you know a Mike Boseman?"

She stared at my chest. Then she shook her head. "Doesn't sound familiar."

* * *

Malcolm and I shared a taxi back into town. He had his sights on the live sex shows in Garibaldi. I wanted two things: to go home and try and clear my name from this fiasco, and to stay longer so

I could spend more time with Flor. But right now, I was bushed. I wanted to catch a solid eight hours of sleep.

The taxi dropped me off on Reforma Avenue. Malcolm continued on toward downtown. I crossed the large avenue and was crossing the next narrow side street about a block from my hotel when a black SUV screeched to a halt in from of me. Two men jumped out. One grabbed me from the side, the other punched me high in the gut. I lost my air, my knees buckled. Before I hit the ground, I was grabbed and shoved into the backseat of the SUV. It sped away, the engine roaring, gravity pulling me back.

One of the men yanked me by the shirt collar and sat me up. Another put a canvas bag over my head, held it tight around my neck. I gasped. Pushed forward. They punched me in the ribs. Again. I doubled over. Tried to breathe. The bag folded into my mouth. I got another punch on the back below my neck. Stars.

I heard something like *"Pinche gringo."* Then something hit me hard on the back of the head. I faded.

I was pulled out of the car, dropped on a hard floor. Someone held me up. I was dizzy. My head throbbed. They pulled the bag off my head. Everything was bright, then dark. A blur. My legs were weak.

"Where is the girl?" There were three of them standing around me in half a circle. The man who spoke had a thick Spanish accent. "Talk."

I nodded, trying to get air, get my bearings.

One of the men stepped forward, swung a right. He caught me high on the cheek, threw my head to the side. My body followed. The man to my side held me up.

"Where is she?"

I shook my head.

Another punch to the side of the face. I tried to raise my hand, but my brain and body were disconnected. I opened my mouth.

Then someone hit me from behind. I fell to my knees, on all fours. I spat. Blood. Nausea.

"Where is the girl?" the man asked again.

"I don't know." It came out of me weak and raspy, like a whine.

One of them kicked me in the ribs. I fell on my side. Coughed, took a deep breath.

"Maya Edwards," he said again. "Where the fuck is she?"

I raised my hand. I gasped for air, shook my head. "She found me," I said. "She came to me. Then she left. I . . . I don't know where she is. I don't know how to find her."

I moved to get up. Another blow to the side. I curled up into a fetal position, hands on my head, arms covering my face.

"I swear. I don't know."

They kicked me like a football. I held on to the words: where is she, Maya, the girl, where. Where. The man's Spanish accent faded.

The kicking stopped. I was lying on my side, curled up like a baby, sides throbbing. Two of the men were in front of me. They were big, dressed in black. But it was too dark to distinguish anything. I couldn't see faces, just shapes. One of them lit a match. His face was momentarily illuminated, yellow, shoulder-length hair.

He lit a cigar. The flame swelled. The end of the cigar glowed red. He tossed the match to the side and laughed. Then he nodded. A man behind me dropped on me, knee on my back, hands on my shoulders, holding me down.

The man handed the cigar to another man. He knelt before me, placed his hand on my cheek, pressed my head down against the ground.

"Now hear this," the man standing over me said, his Spanish accent completely gone. "You go home. Leave Mexico. Don't come back. Now, here's a souvenir for you."

The man holding my face pressed the lit end of the cigar against my ear. The whole side of my face burned. I screamed. He pressed the cigar hard into my ear canal, twisting the cigar like he was putting it out in an ashtray. It was like a bomb had gone off in my head.

They let go. I turned over, brushed my ear, pressed my hand to it, shut my eyes tight against the pain—excruciating.

Someone laughed. I heard shuffling, the car doors closing, engine starting, revving, wheels turning over gravel, fading. Then the car honked the first five notes of "La Cucaracha" somewhere in the distance.

I stayed on the ground with my hand on my ear. Every breath brought pain to my sides. I figured broken ribs. I didn't move for a long time. My ear buzzing, my brain spinning.

After a long while I staggered to my feet. The ground tilted. I was dizzy. Cars in the far distance. Lights. I checked my pockets. I still had my wallet, my cash—but they had taken my cell phone. I walked, one small step after another, unsure of my direction. I was in a field, a long flat field of some kind. Not a park, the country, somewhere in the outskirts of the city.

I walked for an hour until I reached a highway. Cars raced by. No taxis, no people. I started walking on the side of the highway, my hand to my ear. The pain and ringing driving me insane.

Then a car pulled over in front of me. Two men got out. I waved at them. Cops. Mexican cops.

We tried to communicate. I said, "*Asalto. Ayuda.*"

One of them looked at my ear. I thought I heard one of them laugh. I couldn't hear properly. The cars were buzzing past. My head throbbed.

"Hospital," I said. "*Por favor.*"

This they seemed to understand. They helped me to the backseat of their patrol car and drove. I leaned my head back and to the side and closed my eyes. The dizziness was killing me. I was going to vomit. But I held it in. I thought of Flor. I kept seeing her face smiling at me, her fingers running along the side of my face, telling me it was all going to be fine.

* * *

When I woke up, I was lying on a couch in a small room lit by a single fluorescent bulb that kept flickering. There was a large metal desk, a couple of chairs, and a pair of file cabinets. The door was closed, but there was a large window that looked out on a large office.

I sat up. My right hand was handcuffed to the arm of the couch. Every inch of my body ached. My head was pounding. My ear burned. I touched the side of my face, looked at my fingers. Blood.

I was dizzy. I rubbed my side, my left temple. I made an effort to clear my head, collect myself. All I could remember was the beating. The men in the darkness. The man's voice: *Where is the girl?* The back of the cop car.

I could hear someone working on a typewriter, voices, the tinny sound of music coming from a small speaker, maybe a radio. I stretched my head to look out the window into the large open office space. The walls were blue and white. A policeman in a blue uniform sat behind a large desk, engrossed in whatever he was reading. Behind him the Mexican seal of the eagle eating the serpent was painted on the wall, the words *Seguridad Publica*, public safety, in big block letters. At the center of the office a man was typing. Four others were gathered around a small TV. Two cops in uniform were eating at a table in the far corner.

This was no goddamn hospital.

I felt around my pockets. My cell phone and wallet were gone. I pulled at my right hand. The cuff was tight. No way to slip my hand out. I checked the couch, an industrial office throwback to the 1970s. Metal with hard gray upholstery seats. No, I wasn't going anywhere.

I glanced at the desk. A computer, papers, a half-empty Pepsi bottle. My passport, my wallet folded out, my Florida driver's license on top.

I scooched down on the floor to where no one could see me through the window. I dragged the couch across the floor to the front of the desk, reached over, and grabbed the passport and my wallet. Credit cards, license, picture of Zoe. It was all there. But no cash. The goons last night had left my money. I remembered that perfectly. The cops. They had taken my money.

I felt over the desk for a key. Nothing. I reached to the top drawer, pulled it open, searched blindly, feeling for anything.

A paper clip.

I heard men outside. I peeked over the window. Two cops were standing a few feet from the office where I was. I pushed the couch back to its original position and lay down on my side.

I tried to unlock the cuffs with the paper clip. They make it look so easy on TV.

It's not.

One of the cops came in, closed the door. I faked sleep. I opened my eyes slightly. He looked over the desk and back at me. Then he glanced out the window. He pulled a set of keys from his pocket and unlocked one of the filing cabinets. He opened the bottom drawer and produced a fat bottle of Potosí rum. He took a long swig and then put the bottle back in the drawer.

"Ramón." The other cop cracked the door open and poked his head in. "*Nos quiere ver el sargento. Ahora mismo.*"

I wasn't sure what it meant, but the cop slammed the drawer shut and walked quickly out of the office.

He left his keys in the lock of the file cabinet.

I waited a few seconds. Then I glanced over the window. The two cops walked quickly away and disappeared down a set of stairs.

I sat down on the floor and pulled the couch with me to the desk. I reached for the keys on the file cabinet, but it was too far. I pulled the couch as far as it would go. Not good enough.

I looked around the office. I felt woozy. I figured a mild concussion. My ear and my left side just below the armpit hurt the most, maybe a broken rib. Either way, I had to get the keys. I had to get the fuck out.

I shoved the couch between the desk and the wall as far as it would go, but it was still too far—about two feet. I glanced out the window at the office. I turned around and stood on the couch and reached for the keys with my foot.

It took me a few tries to kick them off. They fell on the ground. I grabbed them with my left arm and unlocked the cuffs.

I peeked out the door. The stairs were to my right, about twenty feet. I took a long breath, straightened my back, and stepped out. Each step brought a sharp pain to my side. I walked quietly, casually, like everything was normal. When I reached the stairs, I stopped and leaned against the rail, took a deep breath.

"Hey!" someone yelled. "*El gringo!*"

I took off, two flights down to a lobby. About a dozen people sat in chairs, waiting their turn to face judicial bureaucracy. Everyone raised their eyes. A woman pointed at me, her expression blank. I looked down, blood on my shirt.

There was a big commotion upstairs: chairs scraping the floor, doors slamming, steps coming quickly down the stairs, someone calling, "Jiménez, García. *El gringo!*"

I bolted around the stairs to the side of the lobby and pushed open the door closest to me. It led outside to a parking lot. A young man, probably the lot attendant, approached me and started with some gibberish. I waved him off and ran across the lot to the street.

There was a line of parked cop cars, six or seven of them. I glanced back at the attendant. He was standing in the middle of the parking lot, his arms hanging at his sides, staring at me. Behind him, the door flew open. Three cops ran out.

I took off as fast as I could. But I seemed to move in slow motion, like a nightmare where my effort was useless—a lot of hard work for nothing. My side and head throbbed. The people I passed on the street stared at me.

I kept going to the end of the block, my chest burning. I looked back. The three cops ran toward me, forty, fifty feet away.

I kept going. I turned the next corner and crossed the street. Three green VW taxis were cruising down the road one after the other like a little train. I raised my hand. They zoomed past, didn't even slow down.

I kept moving, walking backward looking for a taxi. The three cops appeared around the corner, moving quickly, looking everywhere. One of them pointed at me. They ran across the street, weaving between the cars. People moved out of their way, stared. They were getting closer.

I turned the next corner. A taxi merged to the side, moving slow. I raised my hand, stepped out onto the street. It pulled over and I hopped in.

"Hotel Maria Cristina. *Rapido!*"

I slouched down on the seat. When we crossed the street, I glanced back at the cops. They'd stopped running. One of them smacked the other on the chest with the back of his hand. They turned and started walking away.

I told the driver to swing by an ATM so I could get some cash. Then I leaned my head back and caught my reflection in the rearview. The side of my face was swollen like a balloon. I had a gash on my left cheek just below the eye. Blood everywhere.

CHAPTER SIXTEEN

I DIDN'T LEAVE my room for two days. I wouldn't let the maid in to clean. I ate room service, downed Motrin every four hours, wrapped my torso tight with one of the bedsheets. I cleaned up my face and ear as best I could. I had a serious cut on my cheekbone and a split lip. The burn in my ear turned to blisters, some of which popped and oozed—red mushy welts that hurt and were at risk of infection.

I didn't bother to update my Maya document. I just lay in bed with a bag of ice on my face, thinking. Who the fuck was trying to find Maya? Who were those men? What did they want with her? I played the events of the night over and over in my head: pushing me out of the car, the questions, the beating, and that souvenir of a smoldering cigar against my ear. The only thing that seemed off was the man who spoke. He had a Spanish accent, but it faded near the end of our encounter. Or maybe the way I heard it wasn't the way it happened. I was scared, beat up. I'd lost proper perception.

They hadn't taken anything from me except my phone. They'd left my passport and my money. Left it for the damn cops. They wanted Maya. They wanted me to leave Mexico. But why?

Hired muscle. They had to be. I was no expert, but I'd heard a few stories, seen enough movies.

But who hired them?

The obvious answer, the one that kept coming back to me and smacking me in the face, was Mike Boseman. It had to be him. He'd freaked when he saw me. But if this was true, then he hadn't hooked up with Maya. They were not an item. They were not in it together. This destroyed all my theories.

Maybe Maya was running away from him, too. One possibility was that Boseman went looking for Maya at Nick's place, killed Nick, and then came to Mexico to find Maya. But why was he after her now?

Unless those goons weren't hired by Boseman.

There were two items hanging in the back of my dizzy head: insurance and inheritance. Maya was the one who had the most to gain, unless she wasn't in Nick's will or named as the beneficiary in his life insurance policy. That's what I had to figure out.

I called Flor and left a message, telling her I'd lost my cell phone and to call me at the hotel. I lay on the bed, watched Mexican soaps on TV, drank some chicken soup, trying to regain my strength. By the third day Flor hadn't called. I imagined she was out, diving in the canals of Xochimilco. I called her again and left another message. I told her I needed to see her. That it was urgent. I wasn't trying to spook her but I was afraid that whoever sicced those goons on me might go after her.

I showered and shaved and went to a pharmacy, bought antibiotic cream for my ear and cheek. I felt better, but I looked like shit. The swelling had gone down some, but my face was a sad cartoon with blue and purple around my eye and lip.

I called Flor again and left her a voice mail, telling her I would wait for her after work at the little café across the street from her apartment in La Condesa.

The first thing I did was go to the Camino Real to check on Boseman.

"Yes, Boseman," I repeated to the desk clerk at the hotel, "Boseman, B-O-S-E-M-A-N."

He worked his keyboard and shook his head. "I'm sorry. We don't have anyone registered by that name."

"Did he check out recently?" I said. "I was supposed to meet him, but my plane was late."

The clerk looked at me for a moment, then he worked his keyboard. "Michael Boseman. Yes. He checked out yesterday."

Well, hello!

I'd had him, but I lost him. The question was what to do next. I looked at the clerk. "What about Maya Zav—sorry, Maya Edwards?"

He took a deep breath and checked for it. He shook his head. "No one registered by that name."

"What about in the last week?"

He grinned. "I'm sorry, but we don't give out guest information."

"But you just gave me Boseman's information."

"I was doing you a favor."

"Can you do me another favor and check for Maya Edwards?"

"I can't do that."

I sighed, pulled my wallet out, pushed a five-hundred-peso bill across the counter. He took the money, smiled, and his fingers danced on the keys again. Then he looked at me, his head tilted to the side. "No Maya Edwards. Sorry."

"All week?"

"Never," he said. "She's not in the system."

I walked away looking at the people: the executives, the businessmen and women, the sunburned Americans. It was a big hotel with a busy lobby. Mike Boseman wasn't here, but things were beginning to gel. Maya and Boseman were not together. Otherwise Boseman would have stayed with Maya. I was almost one hundred percent certain that Boseman was looking for Maya. The question was why. I took a taxi to La Condesa and found a seat outside the little café by Flor's apartment. I ordered a cappuccino and watched the people making their way along the sidewalks, checking the menus posted outside the restaurants. It reminded me of downtown Sarasota. For the first time since I had arrived, I was homesick. The town I loved to criticize was now a paradise in my imagination. There was an order to things. Here, despite the big shade trees and the cafés one after another along the sidewalk, there was a weird anarchy: the cars double parked on the road, mayhem everywhere, the juxtaposition of wealth and poverty. It was unnerving.

My heart was beating fast. My palms were sweaty. Every dark-colored SUV that rolled past spooked me. I was pretty sure I was being watched.

"Dexter!"

It was Flor. She ran to me. "Oh, *Dios mio*. What happened to you?"

"Someone put a cigar out in my ear."

She touched my cheek, her hand floating gently over the cut. "What's going on?"

I came clean with everything. I told her about Nick and Maya and Boseman and the goons from the other night. I just dumped it all on her lap like a dying man making a final confession.

Her eyes welled up. She squeezed my hand. Her lower lip trembled like she was about to cry, but she held it in. I appreciated that. I'm not sure I could've handled her crying or going into hysterics. This whole thing was getting crazier by the day. I wasn't sure how much longer I could remain in control. I had not been able to talk to anyone about the case, if I could even call it that anymore. But talking to Flor took a huge weight off my chest.

We went up to her apartment, and she ran a bath for me, helped me undress. She sat on the floor of the bathroom next to the tub and washed my beaten and bruised body. I closed my eyes and thanked my lucky stars. This was a woman to keep. I was in a place I had wanted to be in all my life, except I hadn't realized that. My stomach tightened when I thought of leaving, of seeing Holly again, that she could ever be as nurturing as Flor.

No matter what, I was going to have to go away, leave Flor. It wasn't that I was scared, although that was part of it. I had to find Tiffany. I had to figure out who killed Nick. And Boseman. I had to find out how he figured into this.

I verbalized my thoughts, my head just over the waterline. "I'm going to have to go home soon."

"Shhh."

"We need to face it," I said.

"I know," she said. "I knew this all the time. And so did you."

"You don't mind?" I was hurt.

"I mind," she said. "Of course I do. But I refuse to avoid things in life just because they might be painful."

I leaned my head to the side and looked into her eyes. I felt myself melting into the water. I hated and loved it—the sweet pain, the wild sensation of gaining and losing all at once.

"I know," I said. "You have to live life."

"I'm glad I met you, Dexter Vega. And I'm glad we've had this time together."

She wasn't sentimental about it. She was a realist. I liked that. I liked everything about her.

"Maybe you will come back soon."

"Maybe you can visit me in Sarasota."

"Sure." She smiled. "Maybe."

I closed my eyes and let the moment sink into me, the smell of the soap and the feeling of her fingers gliding gently over my skin. There were too many maybes in my life. They were like a never-ending echo: maybe. Maybe what I needed was something absolute, something certain. Maybe.

* * *

The following evening, I took a taxi to Toni's place in La Roma. I was early for the dinner invitation, but I wanted to talk with her about Maya. I had to tell her about Boseman. Maybe deep down I had the intuition she would give me a clue, something that would help me figure this thing out.

Her apartment was in an old art deco building. It was large with a lot of windows and looked down on a small park. A maid let me in. The walls were covered with art. An old stereo played a vinyl record of Miles Davis' "E.S.P." I could hear the definition, the dust cracking and popping.

Toni was all dressed up, working in the kitchen with another maid, giving orders, making sure everything was perfect. I don't know what she was cooking but it smelled amazing. When she saw me, she did a double take.

"What happened?" She came to me and placed her hand on my cheek. It's funny how women do that. "Are you all right?"

"I'm okay," I said. "I'm sorry I'm early, but I wanted to talk with you."

"Is this about Maya?"

"Everything's about Maya."

She smiled. Then she gave instructions to the cook and led me out of the kitchen. "Can I offer you a cocktail?"

"Just a beer."

She asked the maid for a beer and a glass of wine. Then she squinted at me. "Someone didn't like you."

I followed her to the balcony and we sat. The windows were open and the sound of the traffic below mixed with the Miles Davis tunes. The maid brought the drinks. She held her wineglass with both hands the way you might hold a cup of hot cocoa on a cold day.

"There's this man," I said. "Mike Boseman. He was in a relation-ship with Maya back in Florida. Now he's here. I'm pretty sure he's looking for her."

"And he did this to you?"

I nodded. "His men did."

I told Toni the whole story. She sat in her chair listening very carefully as if I were giving her a set of detailed instructions on how to save the world. She didn't even take a sip of her wine. She just sat, listening, nodding, her wide dark eyes locked on mine.

When I was done with the story, she gave me a knowing smile and said: "He'll never find her."

I leaned back. The Miles Davis album had stopped playing and I was imagining the needle dancing at the end of the record, waiting for someone to pick it up.

"How do you know?" I said.

"Because I do."

"But you can't be sure—"

"She's gone, Dexter."

"What?"

"She knew this man was after her. She chose to meet with you and set the record straight. Then she left. She doesn't want to be found."

I let it sink in. Toni knew more than she had let on earlier. It pissed me off, but it also reassured me. In a weird way, I knew Maya would be okay. But I still didn't get Boseman's game.

"What's going on?" I said.

"It's exactly like Maya told you. She just wants out of her old life."

"But what about Boseman? What does he want with her?"

Toni shrugged. The doorbell rang and the maid went to the door. Toni leaned forward and touched my knee. "I suggest you leave it alone, Dexter."

She stood and went to meet the couple who had just arrived. I looked out on the little park across the street. I wasn't going to press Toni about what she knew about Maya. It was obvious she knew her better than she had let on. And she had helped me. Perhaps it was better left at that. Maya was free. She knew how to take care of herself. Perhaps Boseman was not as much of a threat as I thought he might be. It was time for me to go—time to face whatever was going on with Nick Zavala's murder back home.

CHAPTER SEVENTEEN

MY HOUSE WAS exactly as I had left it. Mimi the cat was lying on the top of the chaise, soaking in what was left of the evening sun. She was so happy to see me, she raised her head from her comfy spot, yawned, and dropped her head back down. Welcome home, Dexter.

In the morning I met my faithful friend and skinny gay photographer, Rachel, at C'est La Vie, a little French restaurant on Main Street. I owed her for taking care of Mimi and keeping an eye on my place while I was gone. But I also wanted an update on the Zavala case.

We sat inside, way in the back of the divided dining room. I didn't want anyone walking by recognizing me, giving me shit. I ordered the quiche lorraine and a salad. Rachel had an omelet.

She leaned to the side and studied my face. "You're looking good. Especially the thing in the ear. What happened, you piss off a Mexican?"

I grinned. I appreciated her sense of humor, but I was quickly running out of patience. I had too much going on in my head. "So, what's going on with Nick's murder?"

"I don't know," she said, and focused on her food. "No one's been arrested. Jason Kirkpatrick did a brief story about the lack of progress in the case. Quoted Petrillo, mostly. It was all about how it was an ongoing investigation and they were narrowing their list of suspects."

"Narrowing their list. Nice. That's cop-speak for *we got nothing.* Anything on me?"

She spread her arms, fork in her hand. "Why does it always have to be about you?"

"I'm serious."

"Kirkpatrick said there were no warrants out for anyone. Shit, Dexter, you know how they are. In two years everyone will forget about it."

"Not Petrillo. Certainly not that other asshole."

"True. But they need concrete evidence and a decent motive. You know that. The last thing Miller wants is to nab the wrong guy. I think she's up to here with scandals." She glanced at my plate. "You going to eat the rest of that?"

I pushed my plate toward her. "You think they know I was gone?"

She picked the crust of my quiche with her hand. "Who, the cops?"

"No, the fucking painters. Who do you think?"

She pointed at me with the crust. "You're getting paranoid, Dex."

Rachel didn't know about my prints on the penis sculpture. Paranoid or not, I was afraid to get snagged by Petrillo at any moment. I had to find Tiffany.

I got a new cell phone and then I took a drive along Bay Shore. I pulled up across the street from Nick's house. There were no cars, no activity. It was just another peaceful day in the beautiful Sapphire Shores neighborhood of Sarasota. A family rode past on bicycles. In the ocean, between Nick's house and the neighbor's place, a couple of small sailboats glided by in the distance. The salty air, the blue sky, the quiet—it was a real change from Mexico City. I rolled down my window and breathed it all in. And what came across my mind was Flor. Beautiful, smart, empathetic.

I started the engine and drove around the neighborhood. Then I got on the North Trail by New College and drove south. I wasn't sure what I was thinking. I thought maybe I would see Tiffany walking the streets. She didn't strike me as a prostitute, but if she had no money, had been a runaway, and had nowhere to go, she might be out here looking for a way to make some cash.

I drove all the way to Fruitville Road and back up to the airport and back. I saw a man selling drugs. Probably crack. But no Tiffany. This was crazy, driving like this. It wasn't methodical. I thought of Flor searching for the axolotl with her team. They had maps, they had grids. They had a plan. They were extremely methodical. I was doing it all wrong. I would never find Tiffany by wandering around the North Trail. That would be coincidence. That wasn't how it worked. And I knew it.

Then, just as I passed 10th Street, I saw a woman walking alone. I pulled up on 12th Street and waited for her to catch up to me. She was wearing jean cutoffs and a tank top and smoking a cigarette. She looked rough, either a prostitute or homeless. Or somewhere in between.

She came to the passenger side of my car. I opened the window. She leaned in. "What's up?"

"I wonder if you can help me out," I said.

"That depends," she said, and turned to the side and blew the smoke away from my car. "What you looking for, sweetie?"

"I'm looking for a girl. Blond. Her name's Tiffany."

She made a face. "What do I look like?" she said and looked over the car at the other side of the street, and then behind her. Then she stepped back. "Cops," she said and started walking away quickly.

I looked in the rearview mirror. A police cruiser was waiting for traffic to pass so it could turn on 12th. I put my Subaru in gear, took a left on Cocoanut Avenue, and headed north.

Two blocks later, I saw the cop car turn on Cocoanut and speed up behind me. The cruiser's lights flashed. A blip of the siren. I pulled over and put my hands over the wheel. I wasn't black, but I was light-brown. To the Sarasota Police it made little difference. I didn't want to give them an excuse.

I watched the two cops approach my car from behind, each with a hand at their side, resting on the handle of their Glocks.

The one on the driver's side said, "License and registration."

I handed him my documents. He was in his thirties, clean-cut, buff, fat neck.

The other cop came around the other side to the front and then to my side. "Can you step out of the car?" he said. "Hands where I can see them."

I did as he asked. "What'd I do?"

"Turn around and place your hands on the car," he said, pointing to the roof of my Subaru. The other cop was already back in the cruiser checking my documents on his computer.

I put my hands on the roof of the car. Hot. Across the sidewalk, I saw the faces of two black kids in the window of a house staring at me. I smiled. They didn't smile back.

"What'd I do?"

"Soliciting a prostitute," he said.

"What? I was just asking for directions."

The other cop walked over and immediately placed a cuff on my right wrist and pulled my arm back.

"What the fuck?" It hurt my ribs where I'd received the pounding. "You can't arrest me for nothing."

They cuffed my other hand. "Do you have anything sharp in your pockets, needles, knives . . ."

"No."

He shoved his hands in my pockets and pulled all the contents out: change, my wallet. They put it in a baggie. The one cop grabbed my arm and walked me to the cruiser while giving me the Miranda Rights.

I sat alone in the back of the cruiser while they searched my car. Then they locked it up and talked, glancing back at me every now and then. After about twenty minutes they got in the cruiser and we drove to the station. They never told me what they'd arrested me for. I thought of what Brian Farinas had said: say nothing. Besides, solicitation of prostitution was difficult to prove. And they hadn't nabbed the woman. They had nothing. I leaned back in the seat, my hands slightly to the side, the cuffs pinching my skin.

* * *

The Sarasota police station is like a lounge at the airport, clean and comfortable and very modern. They took me to an interrogation room on the second floor. It was small, about six-by-eight feet with fancy metal walls, a pair of new office chairs, a small table, and a video camera in a corner of the ceiling. I sat alone, the cold AC blowing on my face. Twenty minutes later, Petrillo walked in.

"Well, what do you know?" I said. "Did you miss me?"

"We have a warrant for your arrest," he said and sat on the side of the table, trying to act cool like some badass TV cop.

"For what?" I said. I was sure it was all bullshit, but there was a smidgen of doubt in the back of my head. Either way, I wasn't going to let on about a damn thing. My lawyer said not to talk. I didn't.

Petrillo pointed at my cheek. "What happened to your face?"

"I cut myself shaving," I said. "You going to tell me about this warrant?"

He took in a long, deep breath. "You're under arrest for possession of child pornography," he said.

"What are you talking about?" I thought of the two uniformed cops searching my car. They could have planted something.

Petrillo gestured toward the camera, the little black dome in the corner of the room. A moment later Frey walked in carrying a MacBook. He set it on the table and opened it. "Is this your computer?"

I recognized my documents on the desktop. "Looks like it."

"Good," Frey said. "Let's take a look at this." He clicked on a file. In a couple of seconds, a movie started playing. A man and a boy were tying up a girl to a bed. She couldn't have been more than twelve years old. The footage was jittery, slightly dark—amateurish. The girl struggled. The man smacked her in the face. Then he ran his hands over her flat chest. The camera moved to the side to get a better angle. The man mounted the girl, covered her whole body like a blanket.

Petrillo leaned past Frey and shut the laptop. "There's more. A lot more. Some pretty sick shit."

"It's not mine."

Petrillo grinned. "We can put you away for a long time, Vega."

"You know what they do to pedophiles in prison?" Frey said.

I leaned back on the chair. "It's not mine."

"Bullshit," Frey said. "It's your laptop."

"It's my computer, but those are not my files." I kept thinking of Brian Farinas: say nothing. But fuck this. They were framing me. Those were not my files.

"And you know what? We found a lot of kiddie porn in Nick Zavala's house," Frey said. "Some of it matches what's on your computer. You two had something going on, didn't you?"

I shook my head. Then I glanced at Petrillo. "I'm not saying another word until I speak with my lawyer."

* * *

They walked me across the street for booking and I spent the night in a cell. After my first appearance in front of a judge, they set bail. Brian got me out by the late afternoon.

"It's bad," he said as we walked out of the building. "They have the evidence, Dex. How did that shit find its way into your computer?"

We stopped at the hot-dog cart on the sidewalk in front of the courthouse. I was starving. I ordered two hot dogs and a Coke. "They stole my computer—"

"Who, the cops?" Brian was a big guy. He wore dark suits that were too small for him. They looked incredibly tight and uncomfortable.

"A couple of weeks ago someone broke into my house. They stole my computer. Someone must have used it. They put those files in there."

"Did you report the theft?"

I shook my head and took a bite of my hot dog. "I didn't think they would find it. You know how it is. Ninety percent of robberies go unsolved; goods are rarely recovered."

"Jesus, Dex—"

"I was busy."

"So how did Petrillo and Frey end up with the computer?"

"I have no idea." My mouth was full of hot dog, extra mustard. "But what's fucked up is that it has the same porn files they found in Zavala's house."

"Here's the problem," Brian said. "Even if we can prove the files were put in your computer in the last two weeks, or whatever date is written on the files, we can't prove your computer was stolen. They'll just say you put the files in there."

"Maybe they did it."

"Who, Petrillo and Frey? Give me a break, Dex."

"Listen." I wiped my mouth with a napkin and poked him in the chest. "The computer was stolen right after Nick Zavala was killed.

Then suddenly it shows up full of kiddie porn in the hands of the cops. That's too much coincidence."

Brian stared at me. He shook his head. "You think Petrillo and Frey had this whole thing planned from the start? Shit. That's saying they were in on the murder."

"I don't know," I said and lowered my voice. "I don't think it's them. But something's going on because that shit ain't mine."

Brian paid for the hot dogs and we walked across the street to the parking lot. "You got a lot of explaining. What happened in Mexico? Who worked you over?"

"That's another funny story," I said. "You remember that guy who a few years back conned the city into giving him a couple million to bring Hollywood to Sarasota?"

"Yeah, he built a big studio near the airport."

"Michael Boseman," I said.

"And?"

"I think he killed Nick Zavala."

"One thing at a time," Brian said. We got into his Range Rover and turned up Washington Boulevard to go pick up my car at the pound. "We need to figure out this porn case. The State Attorney won't let something like that fly. They're hard-asses with this kind of thing."

"They stole my computer!"

"Who's *they*?"

I turned away, looked out the window. "I don't know."

Brian shook his head. I could tell he was worried. It was rare to see him like this. He was usually so laid back, making jokes. He reminded me of Bluto, John Belushi's character in *Animal House*.

He cranked up the AC and turned one of the vents toward me. "You have an alibi?"

"What for?"

"For the computer. Did anyone know the laptop was stolen? Anyone who can corroborate your side of the story?"

"Holly."

"Holly Lovett?"

"Yeah, Holly Lovett."

* * *

When I got home I showered, cleaned the stink of jail off me. Then I called Holly. She didn't answer, but I left her a voice mail telling her I was back in town and that I needed to see her. "I have a lot to tell you."

I hung up and thought of Flor. I was not going to mention her to Holly, but it was odd how I couldn't think about one without thinking of the other. It made me feel queasy.

I put on Miles Davis, an original first press of *Sketches of Spain,* and lay down on the couch to think.

Mimi hopped on my belly and lay curled up, purring like a kitten. I wasn't sure what to do next. I needed to know what the cops were thinking. I needed to know what they had. Someone was doing a damn good job of framing me. For all I knew the cops could have found Tiffany in the house and taken her in. Maybe she put it all on me. No. She didn't even know my name.

Who the fuck stole my laptop and loaded it with kiddie porn?

I couldn't see Petrillo setting me up like this. He was too smart. He'd been a cop for too long. Besides, despite the fact that we clashed on a lot of things, he wasn't a bad guy. And he was honest. Frey. That was another story. That motherfucker wanted to speed-climb the ladder. I could see him doing everything possible to build a case, even if he had to do a little dirty work.

After a while, I hopped in my Subaru and headed south toward the grocery store. I needed to pick up some supplies, food, booze; but for some reason I kept driving past the Publix. I didn't know where I was going. I just kept going, thinking. I figured maybe something would wake up a memory, spring an idea, put me back on track.

A part of me wanted to come clean with Petrillo. I wanted to tell him about Mike Boseman. But now that they had all this other shit on me, it would look like a diversion, like I was trying to slither out of the way. Besides, I had no evidence to link Boseman to Maya, much less Nick.

I drove down to Siesta Key. I had just turned on Midnight Pass Road and was approaching the turn-off for Point of Rocks when the blue Prius in front of me slammed on the breaks. A silver Buick in the other lane screeched. I swerved off the road to avoid the Prius. A green Mustang and a red VW cut across Midnight Pass and sped back toward town. The man in the Prius gave someone the finger. Classy snowbirds.

I parked in front of Boseman's shuttered house. The silver Jaguar was in the driveway. I sat in my car thinking, but there was nothing to figure out. I knew what I had to do.

I walked to the back, checked the hurricane shutters, every door and window. They were of excellent quality, and all of them were locked.

I went back to my car and took the tire iron from the spare tire kit. I walked around the side again. There was a side door, probably to the kitchen or utility. It was the only one that wasn't covered by a metal shutter. I used the flat section of the tire iron like a crowbar. I jammed it between the door and the threshold above the lock and pushed.

It's not like in the movies. The lock didn't budge. I raised the tire iron a little higher and tried again. A small chunk of the door busted. I shoved the tire iron further between the door and the threshold and pushed. I broke another piece. It was the only way. I slowly tore the door apart. The hinges and locks remained intact. When the hole was big enough for me to slide my hand in, I reached in and unlocked the door.

I listened for the beep of an alarm. Nothing. I checked the wall around the utility room. No alarm. I wiped the sweat from my face with my shirt and made my way through the kitchen, the dining room, the living room. The shutters made the house dark. There was very little furniture. I found the alarm panel in the foyer. It wasn't armed.

I switched a light on and began searching for something— anything. There was nothing personal in the house: no art, photos, papers, clothes. But someone had brought the mail in. There was a stack of envelopes on a chair by the hallway between the living room and the dining room. I flipped through it. Junk mail and advertising flyers addressed to Boseman or current resident. Nothing personal. No letters. No bills.

I went upstairs. The same. No furniture, nothing personal, except the bedroom had a nice four-poster bed with pillows, sheets, and a thick comforter. There was toilet paper in the master bathroom. I checked under the bed and found a pack of Trojan condoms.

I glanced at the large shuttered window. This had to be the room from which Boseman had been looking down at the patio when I first came here.

I went downstairs and looked in the garage. Empty. When I came here before leaving for Mexico, the house had just been shuttered. The Jaguar had not been in the driveway. It could have been in the garage. Someone must have moved it. Or someone was driving it.

Either Boseman was back or he had an accomplice. What I couldn't put together was why he lived like this, in a house with no furniture.

I went into the kitchen. Checked the fancy Sub-Zero fridge. A plastic gallon of water and an open box of baking soda.

I checked the cupboards and drawers. No plates or flatware, no food.

It was useless. I sat on a chair. Maybe Boseman was getting ready to sell the house. But what about the Jaguar?

Maybe it wasn't his.

I walked out the side door where I had come in and walked toward the front. There was a large plastic trash can and a pair of recycling bins next to the AC unit.

I opened the trash. Two big black Glad bags. I pulled one out and tore it open. It stank of rot—of dead animal. I held my breath and sifted through the shit. I found an electric bill and a receipt from Publix. The FPL bill was in Boseman's name and totaled $763.42. The invoice was for three months and was demanding immediate payment. The grocery receipt was for a whole roasted chicken, mashed potatoes, two salad bags, a twelve-pack of Corona, and a bottle of Mirassou wine. Dated four days ago.

I checked the recycle bins. Twelve empty bottles of Corona, an empty bottle of Mirassou wine, an empty bottle of Margarita mix. The other bag was worse. The stench was unbearable. The contents had turned to mulch.

I went to the back, rinsed my hands in the pool, and walked around the other side to the front. I placed my hand on the hood of the Jaguar. Warm. But it could be the sun. I placed my hand in front of the radiator. It was impossible to tell. I checked the tires, ran my hands over them to see if there was a key. I knelt down and checked around the front bumper. Nothing.

When I stood up, a white Grand Marquis was pulling up behind the Jag. Petrillo and Frey got out of the car. Frey pulled out his pistol and pointed it at me. "Okay, buddy boy, hold it right there."

I raised my hands. "I'm unarmed."

Petrillo waved at Frey to put down his gun. It was his official weapon, a Glock 40 and not that Dirty Harry monster I had seen him packing the other day outside my house. Frey pointed the weapon up but didn't holster it.

Petrillo approached me from the left side of the Jaguar. "What the fuck are you doing here, Vega?"

"I was going to ask you the same thing," I said.

"Put your hands down," he said and looked back at Frey standing to the side of the Jag, his Glock pointed up, but ready. "Jesus Christ, will you holster that thing."

Frey put the gun away slowly and walked around the other side of the Jag.

"I was trying to find Mike Boseman."

"He a friend of yours?" Frey asked.

"Sort of." I looked at Petrillo. "What are you doing here?"

"We got a call."

I looked at the neighbor's house. It was shuttered.

"Did you break in?" Frey moved closer, his hands resting at the sides of his waist.

I shrugged and addressed Petrillo. "Who called you?"

"Anonymous tip."

"Right," I said. "But did they call 911 or did they call you personally?"

"That's none of your business." Frey grabbed my arm, turned me to face him. "I asked you a question."

"I was just looking for my friend."

He pushed me against the car. "Put your hands on the vehicle."

I looked at Petrillo. He looked down, kicked the Jag's tire.

I did as I was told. Frey came behind me and frisked me. Then he took my right arm. The cuff zipped around my wrist. Then he cuffed the other. Two times in two days. Unbelievable.

Frey turned me and sat me on the hood of the Jaguar facing him. "Now what?" I said.

He put his index between my eyes. "You stay here."

Frey and Petrillo walked to the back of the house. They were gone for about twenty minutes. When they came back, Petrillo said nothing. Frey grabbed me by the arm and led me to the backseat of the Grand Marquis—didn't even bother to read me my damn rights.

CHAPTER EIGHTEEN

THEY SAT ME down in the interrogation room and shot a lot of questions at me about my relationship with Boseman, about what I was doing in the house, why I had broken in. They brought up the kiddie porn again—threatened me with prison. I told them nothing.

I used my phone call to ask Brian Farinas to get me out. But I hadn't been booked. I wasn't even walked across the street to the jail. I was cuffed in an office on the second floor of the Sarasota PD building. So Brian couldn't bail me out. Instead, an officer escorted me down to the lobby. I could see Brian's big frame by the tall glass windows. "What's the matter with you?" he said and put his arm around me. "Can't you just take it easy for one day?"

"Shit, Brian."

"They didn't abuse you in any way, did they?"

"They gave me coffee," I said.

"First class."

"Vega!" It was Petrillo. "Can I have a word?"

Brian frowned and put his index finger to his lips. "I'll wait outside."

I turned to Petrillo. "Detective."

"Listen, I don't know what's going on. And I know Frey's been a little hard on you—"

"A little?"

"The State Attorney's office is breathing down our necks about the Zavala case. And Chief Miller is right there with them."

"Why?"

"I don't know. Miller's got Frey on a short leash."

I smiled. "They oughta put him in the pound."

"Maybe." Petrillo grinned. "But there's more to it than that."

I crossed my arms over my chest and leaned closer to him. "What's going on?"

"Miller's being considered for a position up north in Beantown."

"Boston? No shit."

"And she's grooming Frey to take over."

"And you're jealous."

"Don't be an ass, Vega. But if Miller leaves for the cold north and she gets her way, Frey'll be running the roost."

Interesting. So Petrillo was getting a little loose with his new partner. Nothing like divide and conquer. "What's going on with the Zavala murder?"

His eyes made a little ballet around the lobby. Then he leaned a little closer. "You're it."

I smiled. I didn't believe him and I wanted him to know that. "So why don't you arrest me?"

"Miller and Frey want all the Ts crossed. No room for error. It has to be solid."

"You know it's bullshit."

"There's another thing," he said and glanced at his shoes. "Miller heard about Frey getting physical with you."

I chuckled. "Who'd she hear that from?"

"Does it matter?"

"I don't know, Detective. You tell me."

"No one's moving on the Zavala case until they know they have a case they can't lose. Everyone up there's watching."

I smiled and looked up. Frey was standing by the glass on the second floor, his hands in his pants pockets, looking down at us like a vulture. I said, "What if I told you I knew who did it?"

"That's bullshit."

"I might. But my information's not free."

He waved his index finger at me. "Look, Vega, if you're withholding information—"

"What? If I'm withholding information, you're going to arrest me? Fuck that shit. Tell me what you know."

"Dexter!" It was Brian. He'd come back into the building. He tapped at his wrist. The cheap imitation Rolex reflected the fluorescents in the lobby. "Let's go."

I smiled at Petrillo. "You're costing me money."

I joined Brian and we walked out of the building and into the blinding, hot afternoon. We crossed the street to the Pane Park parking lot. Three teenagers rushed past us on their skateboards.

Brian walked quickly, his short arms swinging at his sides. "What was that about?"

"He said I was a prime suspect in the Zavala murder."

Brian stopped. "He said that?"

I shrugged. "Not in those words. But Miller won't let them move on it until they have a rock-solid case."

Brian smiled. "They don't want to fuck it up."

"That's what it sounds like."

We started walking again. "So what the fuck were you doing breaking into a house on Siesta Key?"

We got into Brian's Range Rover and started toward my house. "It's Mike Boseman's house."

"The Hollywood guy?"

The AC felt good on my face. I put my hands up to the vents to take it in. "The one and only."

"Go on."

"He was dating Nick's daughter who isn't really Nick's daughter."
He looked at me.

I pointed ahead. "Watch the road, Counselor."

He turned on my street and pulled up by the driveway. "Where's your car?"

"Siesta."

"For real?"

"Don't worry. I'll get a ride."

"We should meet later," he said. "You can bring me up to speed with your new career."

"The pub?"

"Tomorrow?"

I stepped out of the car. "I'll check my agenda and have my secretary give you a ring."

Brian smiled, gave me the finger, and drove away.

*   *   *

I called Holly.

"Where are you?" she said.

"I'm home. Why?"

"I heard you got arrested."

"Bad news travels at supersonic speed."

"You okay?"

"Yeah. Brian got me out."

"Brian Farinas?"

"He's the man."

"Why didn't you call me?" she said.

"You're always busy. Besides, I can't afford your rates."

"Dexter. I would never charge you."

"Thanks." I really meant it. Her words touched me. And I would have called her when Petrillo and Frey arrested me, but Brian was a good friend. I knew what to expect with him. And if I'd called Holly and she didn't answer, well? I would take that kind of thing personally. With Holly, everything was personal.

"So what was it?" she asked.

"What was what?"

"Why did they arrest you?"

I laughed. "Breaking and entering," I said. "But listen. Is there any chance you can give me a ride to Siesta?"

"I can't at the moment. I'm in Lakewood Ranch and then I have a meeting with a client in downtown Bradenton."

"That's fine," I said. "I'll get someone else."

"We can meet later—"

"We'll see. I might be in jail by then."

I called Rachel. "I need a couple of huge favors. One is bigger than the other."

"Ah, Dexter favors. I love Dexter favors. They can be pretty involved."

I laughed. "This one's simple."

"You said two."

"I know. Can we deal with them one at a time?"

"Shoot."

"I need a ride."

* * *

Rachel picked me up an hour later and drove me down to Siesta to pick up my car.

"So what's the second favor?" she said with the kind of good humor that made me feel like no matter what we would always be best friends.

"You keep an archive of all those photos you take at events, right?"

"You mean those stupid fund-raising galas and shit?"

"I was wondering. This Mike Boseman guy has money. He's a bit of a player in town, right?"

"I guess."

"He must have attended some of these galas."

"So you want me to go into my archive and do a search for pictures of Boseman."

"Is it a lot to ask?"

"Not really. With digital files, I have everything captioned and keyworded."

I smiled. "I'll get some wine."

"Wine?"

"Rum?"

She smiled and turned on Point of Rocks. "Fireball. A big bottle. And some Chinese food. Moo-shu pork and fried rice. With shrimp."

She pulled up next to my car. I looked at Boseman's house. "Hello?"

"What is it?" she said.

"The Jaguar's gone."

"So?"

"So it was there earlier today. Fucking Boseman is back or someone has access to his house."

"Dexter . . ."

"Wait here," I said. "Blow the horn like a crazy lady if anyone comes."

"What's going on?"

"I have to check on something."

I ran across the street and went slowly around the side of the house to the broken door. It was exactly as I had left it, but the trash cans along that side of the house had been emptied. And today was not trash day.

I pushed the door open and peeked inside. It was dark like before, shutters still closed, locked. I walked in slowly, quiet. Nothing
had changed. I went past the kitchen, past the living room to the
other side of the house, and opened the garage door. There it was:
the Jaguar.

What the fuck? I touched the hood. No heat from the radiator
area. I wrote down the license plate number. Then I walked out
of the house and ran across the street. I gave Rachel an okay sign,
hopped in my Subaru, and we were off.

I stopped at a liquor store in Gulf Gate, bought two sixes of Big
Top Trapeze Monk—a local white Belgian ale—a big bottle of
Fireball, and ordered Chinese takeout from the place on the corner.

Rachel lived in a one-bedroom apartment on top of a garage in
the backyard of an old house off Osprey Avenue. It was a neat little place, but she always complained about her landlords, always
looking out their kitchen window at who came and went from her
apartment. She said it cramped her style.

When I got there with the provisions, Rachel was already going
through the hard drives connected to her iMac.

I set the food on the table by the kitchenette and put the beer in
the fridge. "Beer or Fireball?"

"Fireball with ice. Tall." She dragged a chair from the dining
room and placed it next to her desk chair so we could both look at
the computer screen.

I popped open a beer for myself and joined her. We searched the
first hard drive for Michael Boseman. Two hits. She double-clicked
on the images. Photoshop opened them to the full size of the screen.
And there he was: Boseman, shiny and smiling at us like the happiest drunk on the planet.

I pointed to the elderly woman standing next to him. "Who's
that?"

"Doris LaPorte. She's a socialite. She's at all these shindigs. You can't have a charity gala or fund-raiser in this town without her. It's kind of creepy."

"Rich people, huh?"

"Not her. She's just a character."

The next picture was the same, but it was Boseman with six other people. No one of consequence. The image dated from the time he was bringing Hollywood to Sarasota. City Councilmen loved hanging out with him. He was everywhere back then.

We went through the other hard drives. Six of them. On the last one there was a photo. It wasn't of Boseman, but he was in it. In the background, slightly out of focus and where the light from Rachel's flash was beginning to fall off, you could see him talking to a woman who had her head turned to the side. It looked like Maya Edwards, but it was difficult to tell for sure. There were two other people talking to Boseman. One of them was clearly Holly's ex-boyfriend, Joaquin del Pino, the accident lawyer. The other man, I didn't recognize.

"When was this?" I asked.

Rachel clicked a link on the drop-down menu and all the information appeared in another window: February 19 of this year. "About four months ago."

I tapped the screen. "You know this guy?"

Rachel slapped my hand. "Don't touch the screen."

She leaned forward and squinted. She shook her head. "I don't think so."

I read the caption. "Fund-raiser for BRAVO, a charity that helps children who are victims of parental and sexual abuse."

Rachel backed away and looked at me. "Good?"

I pulled my chair back and stretched my legs. Took a long drink of beer. "I didn't know we had a nonprofit like that in Sarasota."

Rachel laughed. "We have a charity for everything here. And don't knock it. Their fund-raisers put food on my table."

"You think they're legit?"

"Who?" She pointed at the computer with her glass of Fireball. "Those guys?"

"Yeah."

"Anyone can start a 501c. It's nothing. Just a bunch of paperwork. Raising the money's a whole other story. But if you're connected and you can get Doris LaPorte to attend, you'll do just fine."

I leaned into the computer. The man talking to Boseman and del Pino looked Mexican. Maybe that was their connection to Mexico. But I didn't want to believe Maya was involved in anything shady. If indeed it was shady.

I had two things to look into. The first was Holly. Maybe she would spill the beans on del Pino. I also had to look up this non-profit, BRAVO.

I pulled out another beer from the fridge and sat on the couch. On the wall across from me was a large black-and-white photograph Rachel had taken when we first worked together for the paper. It was a strong portrait of an old cattle rancher in Myakka, a few miles east of town. He was a real cracker. Inherited his ranch from his father who inherited it from his father who was an original homesteader back at the turn of the century. Development had encroached all around him and the taxes on the land were killing him. The photo was taken at dusk. He was leaning on a fence and looking out at something. His eyes had a look of real hurt, but also of resolve. You could see in his face that he'd been through hell and back, and still hadn't given up the fight. The article I wrote and Rachel's photos got him a reprieve. People rallied around his cause and the county made an exception, not just with him, but with a number of older residents who lived on land their family had owned for generations. But eventually, progress prevailed. He had to sell out.

I pointed at the photo with my beer. "Those were the days, eh?"

"Not for him." Rachel sat next to me. We both stared at the image for a long time. The contrast was rich, crisp and full of texture. I loved that photograph.

"I mean, the days when we did good work," I said. "When we still believed."

"Don't be such a cynic, Dex. You still believe. You just don't have a job."

Maybe she was right. The only reason I was in this mess was because of the layoffs, and because I hadn't really bothered to look for another job. She was right. I still believed. Maybe that's why I couldn't help myself, why this thing with Nick and Maya and Boseman refused to go away. But there was also Petrillo and Frey. Those two were closing in on me. And they were going to put this on me if I didn't find Zavala's killer first.

CHAPTER NINETEEN

THE FOLLOWING MORNING, I called Officer John Blake and gave him the license plate number for the Jaguar. He promised to call me back before the end of the day. Next I Googled the nonprofit BRAVO. They had a shitty web page with very little information. Their *about* page only said they were a charity helping children who suffered from abuse. They had a few links to anti-bullying articles and a few pictures of poor children in Mexico or some other place in Latin America. There was a contact page with a PO Box where people could send donations. They had no names, no physical address, no phone number, nothing tangible.

I smelled a rat.

I continued to search. Corporationwiki, a website that tracks all kinds of corporations and their officers, revealed that BRAVO was a domestic nonprofit that had filed for its status last September. It had a state ID number and was active and seemed on the up and up. The only key officer listed was Joaquin del Pino, Director.

That was my lead: del Pino. I called his office, but the receptionist said he was unavailable and put me through a series of questions about the nature of my call—what kind of accident I had, the type of injuries I suffered, and what insurance companies were involved. When I told her I had to talk to him about a different matter, she changed her tone and took my message. "Mr. del Pino will return your call as soon as he's available."

End of story.

Holly Lovett. She was my next lead. She had to know everything about del Pino and probably knew everything about his shady non-profit. I called her and, big surprise, I got her voice mail.

What was it with lawyers and phones?

I drove out to Nick's house, just cruised by, didn't stop. There it was in all its modern 1970s simplicity—dark and full of lies. I needed to find out what was going to happen to the house, his art collection, his fortune, and if there was a life insurance policy. I had seen nothing about that mentioned in the paper or anywhere else. I drove to the Hob Nob to get a bite to eat. The place had just been remodeled, but it retained its casual 1950s drive-in style. I sat outside and ordered a double cheeseburger with extra mustard. Then I called Jason Kirkpatrick at the newspaper. He was smug and full of himself like any twenty-nine-year-old asshole who's being told by the editor that he's a rising star. Been there. Done that.

"What can I help you with, buddy?"

That was a nice touch: buddy. "Listen," I said, "you're the one on the Nick Zavala story, right?"

"Was," he said. "There's nothing to write about. Nothing's happening, buddy. Margaret has me on other assignments. Better stories."

"Let me ask you something. Did you ever hear what was going to happen to Zavala's money?"

"Who would I hear that from?"

"From whoever is handling his estate."

"And who would that be?"

I laughed. "That's why I'm calling you."

He laughed. "No one knows anything. There's been no statement, no release. Zippo."

"But the guy was loaded, right? Someone's bound to inherit his fortune."

"And his life insurance."

"How much?"

"I'm just saying."

"Have you heard anything?"

There was a long silence. Then he said, "You working on a story?"

"I'm just trying to figure out what happened."

"Why?"

"Because."

"You were at the house the night of the murder. Who you working for, Vega?"

"No one."

"You're a funny guy. Full of tricks."

"Come on, Jason."

"I gotta go." He hung up. That little piss-ass motherfucker hung up on me. The waitress brought my food. I dug into that cheeseburger like it was my last meal.

* * *

I drove up and down the North Trail again, looking for Tiffany without a plan, without really knowing why. She probably had nothing to do with Nick other than sex. Maybe she could tell me something I didn't know. But there were no guarantees with her. She probably wouldn't even talk to me. She was tough, took shit from no one. Even if I found her it didn't mean she would spill the beans—if she had any beans to spill.

I went all the way to downtown Bradenton and back. Twice. Nothing.

The heat and the meal and the days were weighing on me. I drove home. I deserved a nap. I checked my e-mail and lay down on the couch with Mimi. Just when I closed my eyes and began to sink into a pleasant and well-deserved nap, there was a knock on the door.

Detective Petrillo.

"Mind if I come in?"

I moved aside. He walked with his hands in his pants pockets, looked around casually.

I spread my arms. "Can I offer you a beer?"

"Sure," he said and ran his hand through his thick mane of hair.

I went into the kitchen, popped open a couple of cold Big Tops. He studied the label.

"Local brew," I said.

He nodded and took a long sip. "Not bad."

I smiled and leaned against the wall.

"Listen." He walked slowly across the living room and sat on the couch. I took the desk chair across the living room.

"I have this feeling you know more about what's going on than we do."

"About what, the Zavala case?"

He nodded, took a long drink of beer.

"And?"

"I know you don't like me." He paused for a moment and looked at the label on the beer again. "You hate cops."

"I hate bad cops."

"Come on, you got a chip on your shoulder—"

"We got one of the worst departments in—"

"Okay, we're not perfect. But we try."

I rolled my eyes. I thought of my father stepping out of the car on that hot dry afternoon outside San Antonio. And the cop with his hand on his pistol, pointing at my father with his finger, telling him to get down. My father raising his hands, getting on his knees, his arms out like Jesus Christ. And the cop . . .

"You forget who you work for," I said, my voice cracking at the edges.

"Yeah? Who's that?"

"The people."

He waved, a nice easy gesture that was as vague as his intentions. "We're not perfect, Dexter. No one is."

I took a long drink of my beer. "Get to the point."

"Frey wants to nail you for the murder. He's playing Clint Eastwood or some shit. I want to nail the real murderer."

"Really?"

"Your prints are on the penis sculpture . . . the murder weapon. It's just a matter of time before Frey and the State Attorney's office build themselves a convincible case."

"The prints are not enough."

He nodded. "Their case is full of holes. But they're patching them up real quick. That kiddie porn on your computer's going to nail the coffin. You know that."

"You asking me to confess?"

He smiled a dry ridiculous smile. "I know you didn't do it."

Now it was my turn to smile. "How do you know that?"

"I've been doing this for a long time. I can tell. You don't have the MO. Besides, the date on the porn files are all the same, two days after the murder. It's obvious it was planted. And then there's motive. I can't place you there. You have no motive. Hell, we can't even connect you with Zavala. And shit. I can see it in your goddamn eyes." He pointed at me with his beer. "You're not a bad guy."

"I'm flattered."

"Don't be."

I fetched us another couple of cold ones. I wasn't sure I could trust Petrillo. He was a cop. I was not a part of the brotherhood. I was an outsider. And, after all I had learned during my reporting, after everything I'd written, I knew I was the enemy. Except to the cops who were really interested in doing the right thing, officers like my inside man, John Blake.

"Tell me what you have on the case," I said. "Everything."

He looked at me and sighed long and slow. "What I told you about Zavala, and the porn, some drugs, but not enough to indicate he was dealing. A few ounces of coke, pot, and a few pills. Oxycontin, Vicodin. Not something that would put him away. So he was a user. Maybe his dealer did it. We don't know."

"Any other prints?"

He looked at me like I had something coming down my face. Then he glanced at his shoes. "Tiffany Roberts. A sixteen-year-old runaway. Originally from Fort Myers. Now in Sarasota. She has three priors with the Lee County Sheriff's office, all drug possession. She also had a prior in Sarasota for prostitution. We picked her up on the North Trail last week and turned her in to Child Services. That's how it works, right?"

"I didn't make the rules."

"Her prints are all over the house, but not in the study where Zavala was killed. Besides, she's a tiny little thing. I can't see her banging his head with that big bronze dildo."

"Tell me something, how did you guys end up with my laptop?"

"Anonymous tip," he said.

"Would that be the same anonymous who called you to tip you off when I broke into Boseman's house?"

Petrillo shrugged. "Sometime last week the computer showed up on my desk."

"Just like that."

He nodded. "Just like that."

"Maybe your fairy godmother put it there."

He spread his arms. "It's how it happened."

"You're a cop. Don't you think it's a little suspicious, a laptop materializing out of nowhere, and then someone calling you about me breaking into Boseman's place?"

"What'd you expect me to do, toss it out? It's evidence."

"You know, for a while I thought it was you and Frey trying to frame me. But now I can see you're too dumb for something like that. Someone's trying to put this shit on me."

Petrillo grinned. "Yeah, who?"

I laughed. "I wish I knew."

"Why don't you tell me what's going on. Why are your prints on the murder weapon?"

I stared at his eyes, waved a finger at him. "Against the advice of my lawyer," I said. "I'm going to tell you something. You're off duty. You're drinking. And you let Frey punch me in the gut when I wasn't resisting, wasn't even looking. You fuck with me, Petrillo, and I will not just have internal affairs rip you a new one, I'll go to the feds. And the press."

"Take it easy."

"I'm not fucking with you. I've done nothing wrong. But you motherfuckers have me running like a rabbit—"

"That's Frey."

"That's both of you."

He raised his hands. Then he set his beer down on the coffee table. It was empty. I figured this was a good time to bring out the tequila. Two glasses. No lime.

Petrillo drank it like a gringo. Shot after shot down the hatch. I sipped. When I put my glass down, he looked at me and sighed like he was expecting a miracle.

"Here's the deal," I said. "I met Nick at a bar a few weeks ago, and he hired me to find his daughter who had been attending New College but had fallen off the map in the last few months."

"She did?"

"You guys were on it."

"No we weren't."

"You looked into it. You dropped the case. There was no sign of foul play. The girl's a woman. Twenty-two. She can do whatever she wants."

Petrillo shook his head. "We'd follow through. Missing persons case. There's no record on Zavala. I looked."

"Bullshit."

He stared at me, his eyes a little bloodshot. No. He wasn't lying. Zavala was.

Petrillo frowned. "Did he pay you?"

"That's my business. But that's why my fingerprints are on that big bronze dick. He was showing it off, asked me to pick it up and feel it's weight."

"What about the daughter?"

"I found out she was in Mexico doing research. When I came to his place to tell him, I found you picking up his dead body."

"And that's it?"

"Pretty much," I said. "But then it got weird. Turns out his daughter's not really his daughter. And she's not doing research in Mexico. She just wanted to get the fuck away. He was obsessed with her. Zavala did some pretty fucked-up shit. Maya just wanted out, so she bailed. Disappeared. Started her own life."

"You think maybe she did it?"

I shook my head. Then I poured us a couple more shots. Nothing like a drunken cop. I smiled. "You know Michael Boseman?"

"The house you broke into . . ."

"Well, he was the fucker who started that Hollywood-Sarasota studio bullshit a few years back, remember that? The city gave him a few million in grant money, and he never did shit with it."

"Yeah, I remember that. The county sued him, then he countersued."

"That's right."

"So what does he have to do with Zavala?"

"It turns out Zavala's non-daughter was dating him."

"So you think he did it."

I nodded. "That's my hunch. He left his house shuttered the day after I came asking questions. Then, when you and that asshole Frey threatened me with pinning the murder on me—"

"I never said that."

"Whatever." This wasn't so bad, coming clean to a cop who couldn't arrest you even if he wanted. "The point is, I went to Mexico to look for this woman, Zavala's daughter. And who do I fucking bump into? Boseman."

He waved his hand left to right. "They're in it together."

"I don't know. But Nick Zavala's a sick motherfucker. Apparently he picked up runaway kids, twelve-, thirteen-, fifteen-year-olds. He took them in and took care of them, cleaned them up, gave them drugs. Had sex with them."

"Tiffany Roberts."

"They were all minors. Tiffany and Maya and who knows how many others."

"That son of a bitch."

"Amen."

Petrillo tilted his head and squinted at me. "You went to Mexico?"

I smiled. "Nick paid me well."

He shook his head. "But this guy, Boseman. Is he still in Mexico?"

"I don't know. He was. Someone's been in his house."

"Who?"

"Fuck if I know. You arrested me, remember?"

"Jesus, lighten up, Vega."

"I'll lighten up when this shit's over."

"So how did you know someone was in the house?"

"Someone's taking care of the mail. They took out the trash, parked the Jaguar in the garage."

I served us another tequila. I could tell he was flying high. But he was thinking. He was trying to put the pieces together. I appreciated that. He took his drink in a shot and grimaced. Then he waved his index finger at me. "What about the motive?" he said.

"Because of Maya. How would you feel if you found out the girl you're in love with had been kept as a sex slave for ten years? I think Boseman found out about Maya's past, went crazy mad, and killed Nick for what he did to her."

He nodded. "Makes sense."

"But there's another possibility: money."

Petrillo perked up. "Money and love. The two deadly motives."

"And self-defense."

"That's not a motive."

"Zavala was rich, right?"

"And then some."

"Who's getting the money?"

He twirled his empty glass on the table like a top. Then he raised his half-closed eyes and pointed at me. "We're looking into it. The old guy'd been through a handful of lawyers and had a very complicated will. They're still sorting it out."

"And his life insurance?"

He smiled and stood. He was a little wobbly on his way out. I stood in the front yard and watched him get in his car. "Two mil," he said before backing out of the driveway. "And it's all going to Maya Edwards."

CHAPTER TWENTY

THE PHONE WOKE me up. It was John Blake. "Dexter?"

"What is it?"

"The license plate belongs to a 2017 Jaguar XJ registered to a Michael Jones Boseman."

"Fuck."

"What?"

"I just thought it might belong to someone else."

"Sorry, man. Anything else?"

"I don't think so."

I took a deep breath. I had fallen asleep early last night. I'd had no calls or messages from del Pino or Holly. To hell with del Pino, I expected that. But Holly? I was beginning to worry about that girl.

I put on Fleetwood Mac's *Then Play On*, from 1969. It was the last album with Peter Green, and kind of broke my heart because it showed where the band could have gone with their music—that interesting limbo between blues and something else, something so new it didn't exist. But it was also a good thinking album. I made a nice breakfast for Mimi and me—fried eggs, bacon, fried potatoes and onions with a generous squirt of Sriracha hot sauce. I served Mimi her dry cat food and put her plate on the table across from me. Nothing like the company of a cat. They don't complain and they leave you alone so you can think.

Later, I sat down at the computer to work on my Maya document. I had to shift my pattern of thinking from finding Maya, to making sense of Boseman killing Nick. If I were a cop, I'd send someone to keep an eye on Boseman's house. But I wasn't a cop. I had no backup.

But I had Rachel.

"No way," she said. "No. I can't spend all day sitting in my car baking like a damn cake. I have to work."

"When you're not working."

"I have like half a dozen assignments to set up in the next couple of days. I don't even know what free time is, Dex."

"Please."

"Why don't you do it? You don't have a job."

"That hurt."

"Dex, don't make me do this. It's so boring. I don't have the time."

"Please, Rachel, just do me a favor. When you're not working, swing by Point of Rocks and check out the house. I'll do the same. If anyone goes in, let me know."

We shared a long dry silence. Then she sighed. "You owe me, man. Big-time."

"I do. I'll get you a nice bottle of Fireball."

"A case."

We hung up. I stared at my document. Maya was getting the insurance money. I imagined she might also get the inheritance. Who else was there?

Maybe Boseman *was* in cahoots with her. They had been dating. She had been living with him. Anything was possible. I couldn't allow my meeting with Maya and her syrupy charm blind me. She could be in it up to her ears. Shit. Maybe she conned Boseman. Maybe she had seduced him and set him up to do the deed. He kills Zavala, she inherits the money and splits. It was so obvious—maybe too damn obvious.

I had to find Nick's lawyer and see who else was poised to get rich from Nick's death.

I called Jason Kirkpatrick and left a message. I was sure he knew who was handling Nick's affairs. Then I called Brian. Lucky me. The first lawyer in the history of lawyers to answer his phone.

"Why?" he said when I asked him about Nick's lawyer.

"I want to know who's inheriting his fortune."

"I thought we were done with this," he said. "I can't keep bailing you out. I work. I have other clients. Come on."

"Just ask around. See what you can find out. Please."

We hung up. He could be so damn temperamental.

I put on another record, R.E.M.'s *Murmur*, and went about cleaning my house and putting things in order. An organized environment allows for organized thinking. Besides, there was nothing else to do. I had the feeling Petrillo was going to lay off my case for a while. He wanted to catch the real killer, and unless Nick Zavala put me in his last will and testament, I was off the hook.

I had to change gears. I had been neglecting my pathetic little freelance business. The money Nick had paid me was going to run out in two or three months. My severance was gone. I had to find health insurance, a job, some way to earn a buck.

I sat down and surfed the net, checking out the job sites. Sarasota had little to offer in terms of work. It was just a tourist spot for rich people and spring breakers. There were two shitty little papers and a couple of fluffy magazines. I hated to think about it this way, but if I wanted to stay in the journalism game, I was going to have to do a national job search. But there were layoffs everywhere—even the *Times* and the *Post*. No one was immune. I had a career that no longer existed. No one was going to hire me. I had to reinvent myself. I had to do something new.

I had three e-mails from the editor of *Sarasota City Magazine*. She wanted some details on my articles cleared up. I shot back with a few exaggerations, the kind of shit she wanted to hear so she could wrap up the issue, send it to print, and mail me my damn check.

I leaned back in my chair and looked at the picture of Zoe I had propped in the back of my desk. I had taken it last year when she was here for the summer. She looked cute. But I remembered the day. She'd been upset because I sent her to day camp while I went to work. I made a mental note to change things. For some reason it made me think of Maya and Tiffany. What they had probably been through. I made a promise to myself, to Zoe. I was going to be more involved in her life.

I picked up my phone and dialed her mother's number. But I couldn't bring myself to press send. What was I going to tell Zoe?

I set the phone down, pushed the guilt out of my mind. I had to finish the business at hand. I would call her later. And I would listen. I would sit there and hear all the stories she had from school and the neighborhood and her grandmother's place. But first I had to sort this out.

One thing that kept plaguing me was Mexico. If that crazy Malcolm could make it as a freelance journalist, so could I. I could put my house up for rent, sell all my shit, and get down there. I could see Flor and freelance for national publications. Who knew? In Mexico the possibilities were endless. Maybe I could even search for my extended family. Or I could move back to Houston or San Antonio. Sure, I had ghosts all over Texas, but I'd be closer to Zoe. I'd become a part of her life.

There was nothing tying me to this place except the house. And Holly. Holly who hadn't called me back in two days and who really might not even give two shits about me after all. I thought of our meetings at Caragiulos and here at home, her hands caressing my hair, her lips, red and shiny with that bright neon lipstick. I loved her lips. I needed to see what was going to happen with that before I could make a move. I wasn't going to mess it up like I did three years ago. No more what-ifs.

But I was getting ahead of myself. I was getting neurotic—full blast neurotic. I could see a wide-open future but didn't know which direction to take. This was the kind of shit that happened when I was idle, when I wasn't elbow deep in an investigation of some kind. Idle time breeds mischief. It drove me to drink. I realized that now. When my mind wasn't focused on something, I was dangerous. I could trip right into a bottle of booze. *Careful, Dexter,* I told myself, *tread with care. Keep your head together.*

I needed to get out of the house. I needed air. I needed to find Joaquin del Pino and learn about this nonprofit and whether Boseman was somehow connected to it.

I drove downtown to his office across the courthouse. It's funny about lawyers. Everyone talks about how much money they make, and I know del Pino made out just fine cheating people out of half the money they were awarded in a lawsuit settlement. Things were fucked up that way—I guess that's why insurance companies and lawyers are a breed unto themselves. But del Pino's office was pretty humble and straightforward. He had a secretary, two paralegals, and a waiting room. Nothing fancy. The furniture was mahogany veneer, and the walls were lined with dark leather-bound law books.

I asked the secretary for del Pino.

"Yes, of course," she said in a gentle tone. "Do you have an appointment?"

"Not really," I said and glanced down the hall at one of the paralegals talking to someone who was out of my line of sight. "But I left a message yesterday."

"Your name?"

"Dexter Vega."

The secretary didn't seem to react to my name. She checked her calendar and a list of names on a book that I imagined were either the appointments or messages for the big-shot lawyer. Then she raised her eyes at me and said, "And when did you call?"

"Yesterday afternoon."

She shook her head as her fingers traced the names on the paper in front of her. I glanced to the side. The paralegal had vanished. The hallway was empty, the doors closed.

"I'm sorry, Mr. Vega. I don't see anything here with your name on it," she said. "Would you like to make an appointment?"

"Sure." I smiled. "But where's Mr. del Pino now?"

"He's in court."

"I see."

"The first opening I have available is on the twenty-eighth."

"That's three weeks from now."

"I'm sorry," she said. "We're very busy."

"But in the commercials he says he'll see us immediately, talk to us in person."

"Were you in an accident?"

I thought of my entire life as one long continuous wreck. "Yes. Pretty bad. It was the other guy's fault. The cops gave him two citations. I keep getting this pain in my lower back—"

"One moment," she said and stood. "Let me speak with his paralegal and see if she can speak with you."

"But the commercial said I'd get to speak with him. You know, Justice for All?"

She covered her mouth. I wasn't sure if she was laughing at what I said, that I said it, or just about the stupid commercial. "Let me see if we can fit you in. Please wait a moment."

She walked down the hallway and knocked on a door. I followed her. When the door opened, I peeked in. No del Pino. His paralegal didn't seem to be bothered by my presence. I held my lower back and winced. The secretary explained my predicament. The paralegal smiled and said she could fit me in first thing in the morning.

"He wants to see Mr. del Pino," the secretary explained. I nodded with a sorry and painful expression.

"I'm not sure he can," the paralegal said. She was very pleasing and polite. I liked her right away. "But I'll talk with him. If you come at seven thirty tomorrow morning, he might be able to duck in and see you before his other appointments."

This sounded vague enough to me. When I left del Pino's office, I walked across the street to the county courthouse. I went through the metal detector in the lobby and asked the officers if they'd seen Mr. del Pino.

"If he's got court, he could be upstairs. I just started my shift," the one officer said.

I took the elevator, passed the next metal detector, and asked for del Pino. The three officers manning the metal detector conferred with each other. Then the female officer said, "He's probably on the next floor. Civil court."

I went up to the next floor, passed the metal detector. Just then a door opened, and half a dozen people walked out of a courtroom, all in suits, all looking prim. One of them wore a neck brace and had an arm in a bandage. Leading the group was del Pino himself.

"Mr. del Pino," I said. They had come to where I was to take the elevator. "Can I have a word with you?"

I'm sure he recognized me. "I'm with a client," he said seriously. "Why don't you stop by my office and make an appointment."

He was so goddamn proper I wanted to squeeze him to death. What Holly ever saw in this yahoo was beyond me. He was short and balding and had deep brown eyes that held no emotion what-soever. He looked dead.

The elevator opened and a few people, all suits, got off and del Pino and his gang got on. I jumped in with them, squeezed shoulder to shoulder. I smiled. "We're like sardines," I said.

No one laughed.

I addressed del Pino: "I saw you're the director for BRAVO. You like to help abused children."

"That's right."

"Do you know Michael Boseman?"

He shook his head. "Please. This is not the time. I'm with a client."

"I know," I said. "But this will only take a second."

"I don't know Mr. Boseman. Not that I can recollect."

"I'm sure you know him. He was at a fund-raiser for your charity at the Ritz-Carlton in February. Does it ring a bell?"

Del Pino smiled nervously and looked away from his client and then up at the numbers on the elevator. The descent was slow. But I was sure it was moving a lot slower for him.

"Of course, I remember the fund-raiser. But I met a lot of people that night. If you make an appointment, I'm sure we can—"

"So it's going pretty well?"

"The charity?"

"Yes."

"It's a lot of work. Not many people know about the abuse these kids suffer."

"What about Mike Boseman?"

The elevator doors opened, and we stepped out to the lobby. I kept pace beside del Pino and his clients. "He was a big shot in town," I said. "He was going to bring Hollywood to Sarasota. Remember that?"

He shook his head. One of his clients looked at me. "I remember that guy."

"There you go," I said. "So, he was at your fund-raiser. And Maya Zavala or Edwards. Do those names ring a bell?"

"Maybe," del Pino said. "Were you there?"

"Unfortunately, I missed that one." We walked out of the building. We were standing on the sidewalk waiting for the light to change so we could cross and go to the parking lot or to del Pino's office. "But there's a great picture. Came out in the social pages of *The Sara-Scene Magazine*. You know it?"

He didn't answer. The light changed. We walked together.

"In the photo you're talking to him. You and Boseman," I said. "Or maybe I should ask Holly."

He stopped walking and turned to face me. "Is that what this is about? Holly?"

"No, no. I'm over all that. Are you?" I had hit a nerve. When someone falls into that space that's full of emotion—that middle ground of fear—they can misstep.

"Listen to me, Mr. Vega." He waved his finger, his face red and moist with sweat. "You cannot accost me this way, in front of my clients, and accuse me of anything."

"I'm not accusing you of anything. I'm only asking if you know these people."

"I told you I do not know them. I do not know any Boseman or Maya whatever the last name was. I don't. If they were at my fund-raiser, that was their choice. I don't know them. I do not know them."

And like that he turned and marched off with his client and their small entourage. Well, he had given me something. He repeated that he did not know them—five times. A long time ago I learned that if someone repeats something, they're probably lying.

I got in my Subaru and drove back down to Siesta Key. I figured I might as well keep an eye on Boseman's house. I parked across the street in a tiny patch of shade offered by a sea grape tree in the neighbor's yard. It was a long shot. Everything was a long shot. If del Pino wasn't willing to tell the truth, then I couldn't count on what he really knew. He was a pro. I couldn't force it out of him.

I was out of leads. And as long as the case stayed open, I was a suspect in the eyes of Frey and the Sarasota PD. I didn't want to go to prison. But it was more than that. I believed in doing the right thing. Zavala and Boseman and del Pino, they represented everything that was wrong with the world. They took advantage of people. They were greedy rats.

I sat sweltering in the car despite the shade. I checked Facebook on my iPhone. Flor was moving her team to a new canal in Xochimilco. She posted a few photos. She wore the wet suit without the mask. Her hair was wet, her eyes focusing on the camera lens—determined and proud. She was surrounded by her team. It was great to have a purpose in life, something worth fighting for. When I was a journalist, I'd had the same excitement. I believed. But my drive to fix the problems of the world was fading fast. I turned on Pandora and listened to some old jazz and stared at Boseman's place. Between the houses I could see an occasional beachgoer climbing through the rocks to get to the other side of the beach. Paradise. But even paradise had its problems. The world was one big problem. I kept telling myself it wasn't my job to solve it. I needed to accept things for what they were. I envied the people who were content living in a cubicle in some office, pushing papers or entering data into a computer. Work was work, and time out of work was time out of work. They didn't obsess about the shit I obsessed with. Living with my brain was exhausting.

I wished I were back in Mexico. I could be with Flor right now, helping her look for the axolotl. But Mexico had problems. Big fucking problems. How could I complain? I swallowed my anger and let it go. Life was not easy.

After an hour or so I decided to call Holly. This time she answered.

"I've been trying to get a hold of you for three days," I said.

"Hey, now." Her tone went from soft, to professional, to downright nasty. "Don't you talk to me that way, Dexter. I've been busy. I work. I have responsibilities."

"I'm sorry, I—"

"You don't have exclusive rights over me."

"I apologize." I took a deep breath, eased up. "I was worried. I thought something happened."

"Well, I have a huge caseload I need to deal with," she said. "This is really not a good time."

"I need to talk with you. It's important."

"So's my work, Dexter. It's going to have to wait."

Damn. She wasn't even calling me Dex. In a strange way it reminded me of del Pino's pissy attitude when I asked him about Boseman. What was it about lawyers?

I didn't want to ruin my chances with Holly. I needed to take it easy. I knew I had a tendency to rush people, corner them. I could be obsessive and that pissed people off.

"Look," I said. "I'm sorry. I guess we're both under a lot of stress. Can we meet for drinks later tonight?"

She sighed. "That would be nice."

"How about Caragiulos?"

"No, no. Let's go somewhere far from downtown. I need a break from this place."

"Shit."

"What is it?"

"I forgot." Brian Farinas. I have to meet him at Shakespeare's pub tonight. "I made an appointment."

"Oh, Dex. Not tonight."

"Let me see if I can get out of it," I said. "I'll call you in a bit."

"I'm meeting with a client in five. Text me, or call me later. After seven."

CHAPTER TWENTY-ONE

BRIAN WOULDN'T LET me off the hook. He was a busy lawyer and had made time for me so we could have a couple of beers at Shakespeare's and discuss my case. I texted Holly and apologized— offered her a rain check. Then I drove out to our little English-style pub in a strip mall just off Siesta Key.

I took a table in the back. It was dark, secluded. There was a good crowd, and it took me a while to get a pint of Guinness. Not very imaginative, but it was really what I was craving, something heavy and smooth.

About fifteen minutes later, Brian showed up, a bottle of Holy Grail Ale in his hand. "I've been looking all over for you."

I raised my beer. "I've been here."

He sat down and didn't waste any time. "So they might be willing to drop the breaking and entering charges if they don't hear from Boseman. But the child porn in your computer is another matter. You need a solid alibi for that one. Otherwise you're going to see some serious time."

"I will."

"That new detective, Dominic Frey, is really making a big stink over you. He says you're guilty and everyone's sabotaging his hard work." Brian took a long pull of his beer. "What'd you do to piss that fucker off?"

"I'm not sure." I stared at my glass. The foam of the Guinness was so smooth and brown like the crème of the cappuccino I had outside Flor's apartment. I missed Mexico. I missed Flor.

"Well, let's not worry about that now," he said. "Frey needs to convince Chief Miller and the State Attorney's office that he has a solid case. They're taking it slow because they want this thing to stick, use the child porn to hook you to the murder, which leads me to ask, how are we with that thing?"

"Not so good."

"I don't know how you get mixed up with these people: Zavala, Boseman, Frey."

"I'm unemployed."

"What does that have to do with anything?"

I shrugged. "Anything on the inheritance?"

"Right." Brian took a long swig of beer. "You're not going to believe it."

"What?"

"Justice for All."

"What?"

He nodded, a wide smile on his face. "Joaquin del Pino is the official executor of the will. He's Zavala's lawyer. Well, one of his lawyers. But he wrote the will."

"But he's a fucking accident lawyer, not a contract lawyer."

Brian shrugged. "One-man band. You pay it, he'll do it. I do all kinds of shit. Look at me now, talking to you and drinking beer."

"That requires some serious talent."

He took another long pull at the bottle, his eyes on mine. "Indeed it does."

"Did he tell you who's getting the money?"

Brian shook his head. "I made the inquiry. They should be getting back to me tomorrow."

I thought about it for a moment. "Isn't that like a conflict of interest?"

"I'm off duty."

"No, for del Pino."

Brian grinned. "I'm a criminal lawyer, but I do divorce and accident cases if it pays."

"But you don't do contracts."

"I could if I wanted to."

"Some profession," I said. "Where are the ethics?"

"Sarasota's a small town full of lawyers. It's dog-eat-dog out there."

"You sound like Rachel."

"Rachel who?"

"A friend. A photographer. She does it all."

"It ain't easy, my friend."

I went to the bar and got another round, only this time I had a Belhaven Ale. I ordered another Holy Grail for Brian and came back to the table.

He stared at my beer. "How come you didn't get me one of those?"

"You didn't ask."

"Some friend."

"So here's something weird," I said. "I found out del Pino is the director of a nonprofit that helps abused children."

"What's so weird about that?"

"He holds Zavala's will. Zavala was a pedophile. And he has a charity that helps Zavala's victims. Weird, no?"

"I guess. But maybe del Pino didn't know about Zavala's nasty perversions."

I shook my head. "Or he would have gone to the cops."

"In theory."

Brian had a good point. The thing that got me was that the thread of possibilities—of who might be guilty of killing Zavala—was getting longer. What had seemed obvious early on was getting murkier by the minute. I thought of the axolotl in the canals of Xochimilco and what Flor had told me once, that the deeper she went in the water, into the places where the axolotl was more likely to dwell, the more difficult it became to see clearly. The same was happening to me and my pathetic search for Nick Zavala's murderer.

"Let me ask you this." Brian pushed his chair back and stretched his legs. "Why are you still investigating the Zavala murder?"

I looked down at my beer, at the coaster on the table. Budweiser. Why do they have Budweiser coasters in the pub? Why was I still all jacked up on this bullshit?

"I think you need to let it go," Brian said quietly. "Let the cops figure it out. I'll get you clear of the two charges. You'll be good."

I shook my head. "I can't." I raised my eyes and traced the tiredness in his eyes. "It's eating me in here." I tapped my chest. "I have no job, Brian. I need something to do. And I feel like I have the answer to this thing on the tip of my tongue. I can't just let it go. I want to know. Shit. I have to know."

"You'd never make a good lawyer."

I laughed. "Neither would you."

We raised our bottles, the bottom of them touching gently in a friendly toast: "To the good guys."

We drank a couple more beers. This time Brian had a Belhaven and I had a Black and Tan. I thought of all the evenings Brian and I had stayed up sifting through documents I'd gotten on the Sarasota PD through the Freedom of Information Act and from a couple of inside sources. We went over every line together, trying to find the bad apples, making a spreadsheet of the times they had used excessive force or charged an innocent person, shot the wrong perpetrator. It was a lot of work—tedious and detailed and time consuming.

And Brian was getting nothing out of it. I might get an award. I got my paycheck. But all he got was the satisfaction that we were doing the right thing for the people of Sarasota.

And in the end, after all that work and exposing the department of multiple wrongdoings, the voters went to the polls and did absolutely nothing. Brian and I got so drunk after that. The city government refused to implement any changes to the department. It had all been a waste of time. We still had the same idiots in charge. The citizens of Sarasota preferred an arrogant and abusive police force. Sad. They deserved what they got.

We had dinner at the pub. I had a hamburger with caramelized onions and brie. Brian had the special, braised lamb shank. Just another night in our lives, so much like all the others, fighting the same useless battles, trying to figure ourselves out as much as we were trying to figure out the rest of the goddamn world.

Later, as I drove home, I thought about checking out Zavala's house or going to Point of Rocks. But it was useless. What was the point?

I went home, parked in my driveway, and walked to the front door. Holly was sitting alone on the front porch.

"Damn!" I hopped back. "You scared the shit out of me."

She stood and put her arms around me and kissed me on the mouth like an old lover. She pushed back and looked at the side of my face. "What happened?"

I smiled. "Long story."

"Jesus." She stared into my eyes, studied the cut on my cheek, my ear, my face. Then she rested the side of her face against my chest and sighed. "I am so tired, Dex."

"Let's go inside," I said and opened the door. "I'm sorry about the dark porch. The bulb blew when I was in Mexico. I haven't had time to change it."

Mimi came to us, rubbing against our ankles. Holly picked her up and held her to her face. Holly had been with me when I adopted Mimi from the pound. I had been doing a story for the paper on the Humane Society's mobile adoption truck and kind of fell in love with the cat—just as I had fallen in love with Holly.

"Would you like a drink?" I said.

"You have wine?"

"Beer or tequila," I said and went into the kitchen.

"God, Dex. You haven't changed."

"Is that a beer?"

"Might as well."

I opened a Big Top and served myself a tequila. We sat on the couch. Holly flicked her shoes off and folded her legs under her. "It's been a long, crazy month."

She was wearing a colorful sundress, something I imagined her wearing out to the farmer's market on Saturday morning. She looked so good, fresh, beautiful—and tired. Her hair smelled great, and she had very little makeup, and glorious bright red lipstick that matched the red hibiscus flowers in her dress.

"You're telling me." I ran my hand along her arm to her shoulder. She leaned her head back and closed her eyes. "You working on a case?" I asked.

She laughed. "If it was only that. I'm in the process of moving my things out of Joaquin's place, and he's being difficult."

"He doesn't want you to leave?"

"I don't know what he wants. He's just being a jerk about it."

I wanted to tell her I had seen her ex-boyfriend, that I was curious about his relationship with Zavala and Boseman. I wanted to ask her if she'd been at the charity fund-raiser at the Ritz. She would know if Boseman was friends with del Pino. But I said nothing. It didn't seem like the time to bring it up and spoil the moment. I had learned my lesson well. My obsessions were not the obsessions of others. They turned people off, drove them away. If I wanted to be with Holly, I needed to back off. Like Rachel had said, don't crowd a woman like Holly.

I put on Chet Baker's *My Funny Valentine*. It had been my first jazz album ever. It had been expensive at the time. An original first pressing. Great sound. The texture of the man's voice, of his trumpet, came out like a dose of heroin. It got me hooked.

I refilled my glass and brought Holly another beer. She moved back a little on the couch, stretched her legs, laid them over my lap, her skirt hiked up almost mid-thigh. I caressed her shins. Massaged her feet. Ran my hands up her thighs. She sighed and placed the beer can on the coffee table. Then she reached for my arm and pulled me toward her, opening her legs, making room for my body. Soon my lips were over hers, pressing against the bright red I loved so much.

* * *

The following morning, I made coffee and put on the Beatles' *White Album*. Holly looked fantastic. I loved seeing her hair ruffled up, messed up over her head. Her sleepy face, eyelids half-closed, and a little cranky at having had to wake up and face another day.

"You have a nice life," she said and served herself a cup of coffee. We went outside on the front porch and sat on the rockers. Across the yard the sun hit my neighbor's oak tree, thick clumps of Spanish moss dripping from its branches like festive decorations. The birds, mocking birds and cardinals and woodpeckers and scrub jays, all over the neighborhood were causing a racket only they could comprehend.

"If you really knew my life," I said, "you wouldn't say that."

"Come on." She smirked. She looked stunning in my button-up oxford. "You have no real responsibility. And you know how to enjoy your environment. I've always loved your house. It fits you so well."

"An old creaky house for a cranky old guy."

She sipped her coffee. Then, without looking at me, she said, "So tell me about Mexico."

The first thing that came to mind was Flor. It flooded me with guilt. Then I thought of the beating, the cigar in my ear. Maya. Boseman. "It was okay."

"Yeah? Was it work?"

"Kind of."

"Was it that thing, looking for the girl? Maya . . ."

"Yeah."

"Did you find her?"

I chuckled and drank my coffee. "You could say that."

"What happened?"

I leaned forward and showed her my ear. "I was asked to leave the country."

"She did that?"

I shook my head and set my cup down. "Someone else did."

She said nothing more, but looked ahead, her hands around the cup despite the warm morning. And I thought of how beautiful she looked, how I had wanted my life to be this moment—me and her together on the porch of this little old house forever.

But I could tell it wasn't for her. This was not her dream. It wasn't even her reality. For the first time in all my years of wishing Holly and I would get back together—make a serious go at it—I saw she would not be happy like this. Not here. Maybe she liked how it looked from the outside, from the visitor's point of view. But not from the inside. It was different living it day in and day out.

I don't know if it was this realization, or if it was something else, but I jumped right into it. "Did you know your ex-boyfriend wrote the last will and testament for Nick Zavala?"

"No, I didn't," she said flatly. "We never talked about work."

How could two lawyers be in a relationship, live together for three years, and not talk shop? I didn't believe her. "I saw him yesterday," I said. "I asked him about his nonprofit, BRAVO."

"I'm surprised he gave you the time," she said.

I laughed. Then I stood and took her cup and went inside. I turned the record over and got us a refill. When I came back, she was standing in the yard looking up at the young oak at the end of the yard. "There's a woodpecker up there. I can see him."

"I know. I hear him every morning."

"That's amazing," she said and came back to the porch and took the cup from me.

"You think del Pino knows Mike Boseman?"

She turned away. "Mike who?"

"Boseman. The guy who was going to bring Hollywood to Sarasota."

"I don't know. Maybe. Did you ask him?"

"I did. But he said he couldn't remember."

"Maybe he doesn't." She turned back and gave me a look, her eyes tired but awake. "I'm going to have to get going, Dex."

"Sure." I was surprised at how sad I sounded. "I saw a photograph of del Pino and Boseman at a fund-raiser at the Ritz."

"Oh yeah?"

I followed her inside. She set her cup on the kitchen counter and went into the bedroom, picking up her clothes, one piece at a time: panties, bra, dress, open-toe pumps. She stopped by the bathroom and looked back at me. "I have to get ready."

I backed away. I paced in the kitchen. In the living room. I went outside and came back in. I changed the record. I put on Lester

Young, *Live at Birdland*. It wasn't a collector's album, just a good album. Good morning music.

When Holly came out of the bathroom, she looked as good as always, just like she was when I found her sitting in the rocker on the porch last night. It killed me to see her, to be with her, to feel such an intense attraction.

"Do you remember that night at the Ritz?" I said.

"The fund-raiser?"

I nodded.

"I go to one of those events just about every month, Dex. They all blend in after a while."

I walked her to her VW and opened the door. She touched my cheek with her hand, held it there like a token, a kiss between friends, love that isn't real love, tenderness without commitment.

"Am I going to see you later?" I asked.

"Sure. Call me."

"I had a great time, Holly. I know you did, too." I don't know why I was saying it, why I was pushing for something I knew was doomed if it was even possible. "We should spend more time like this."

"Sure. That would be nice." But I could hear an empty echo ringing in the hollowness of her words.

"Can you do me a favor?" I said. "Is there any way you can find out from Joaquin who's inheriting Zavala's estate?"

"Didn't you just tell me you found Maya?"

"Yeah, but—"

"Look, Dexter. First of all, it's a private matter. Joaquin is bound not to divulge unless his client releases him. Second, I am not really on good terms with him anymore. I don't want to talk to him unless I have to."

I took a step back. "I was just asking."

"Why are you going on with this?"

"It's who I am, I guess."

She waved a thin, red-nailed index finger at me. "That's the thing. You don't know when to let go. That's what makes you miserable. That's why we can't be together. You can't just let things lie."

"I'm naturally curious. I can't help it."

"Well, you should try." She got in the car and closed the door. She backed out and then opened the passenger window and leaned over, her dark butterfly-shaped glasses hiding her big green eyes. "Please try and grow up, Dex. Take responsibility for your own path in life."

Then she drove off.

CHAPTER TWENTY-TWO

I HAD TO push the Zavala case aside for a while. The editor of *Sarasota City Magazine* had been hounding me about the fixes to my copy. She said they were getting ready to go to print and needed this wrapped up yesterday. The changes I had sent her helped, but they didn't go far enough.

I sat at the computer and began to rework the article. More adjectives, more adverbs, and more details about the marble floor in the bathroom, what kind of marble, what kind of fixtures. Was it a Whirlpool tub? Did they have his and hers closets?

It was amazing to see the kind of shit people cared about. A faucet was a faucet. The only bad faucet was the one that leaked. But I couldn't say that, so I closed my eyes and tried to remember the fucking opulent and over-the-top fixtures in the master bathroom. Gold. They were tacky gold-plated faucets. But now I had to spin that into pretty talk for the readers of the seven-dollar magazine that was like a long real estate ad.

I wrote: *The master bathroom was a jewel in itself. The silk smooth Greek marble invited the soul to indulge in the finest Italian handmade, gold-plated faucets that reflected every sparkle from the vanity lights and made you wonder if you were in the presence of the gods. Beauty is too small a word for what the designers have accomplished with this unique and opulent space. This house was designed with the most luxurious details for the ultimate pampering of its owners.*

There. Good enough to make me puke. I was on a roll. But then I was interrupted by Maya. It just crashed against my brain like a dream you forgot you had. A déjà vu—Holly. When we talked this morning, she asked me if I had found Maya. How did she know her name? I thought back to all our conversations. I was pretty damn sure I'd never mentioned Maya. Someone else could have mentioned her name. But who?

I made a mental list: Nick Zavala, the hippies, Boseman, Petrillo, Frey, Brian Farinas. No one else knew unless del Pino knew something I didn't know. He could have told Holly. Maybe that was it. So the motherfucker did talk about his clients, and he must have mentioned Zavala's will to Holly. And maybe that business was who gets the inheritance: Maya.

I had to confront Holly. There had to be a connection. She was a good lawyer. She helped poor people. I must have missed something. Maybe it slipped my lips, which was possible. I could have said something when I was still swimming in the haze of my post-layoff binge. Or del Pino. Del-fucking-Pino. It had to be him.

I needed to think about that. But for now I had to push it aside. Focus on my home and real estate stories for the magazine. I put on Coltrane's *Live at the Village Vanguard*. Cranked it loud, and typed away like a secretary in love.

When I finished, I e-mailed the story to the editor and drove out to Bird Key where del Pino lived. Where Holly lived—until recently.

There were no cars in front of the house. I sat in my car, windows open, salty breeze passing through, filling my lungs, energizing me and clearing my mind of clutter. Del Pino. That motherfucker was deep in it. Something had always been fishy with that guy and his Justice for All slogan. He had managed Zavala's will. And maybe his nonprofit was something he'd done to clear his conscience for it.

Crap. But how would he know about Zavala abusing young girls? He would have gone to the cops. He couldn't be that fucked up.

Or maybe he was.

Sonofabitch. All this time I had been focusing on Boseman when it was probably del Pino.

I wasn't sitting there more than twenty minutes when I realized this was ridiculous. It was Thursday afternoon. Del Pino was at work. He wouldn't be back until evening.

I drove out to Zavala's house. There was no activity. Nothing. I parked at the end of the block and looked back at the house through my rearview mirror. I don't know what I could get out of that place if I could even get in. Still, I waited. Maybe deep down I was thinking of Tiffany. If I was, I didn't know it then. I just sat in my car looking back at that sleek white house with the small rectangular windows and the neat wooden door.

Fuck. How some people lived. How the lucky, the corrupt, the sick, the cheaters, and the liars made their way in this world baffled me. How did good, honest people ever make money? And I mean above and beyond that upper-middle-class place people refer to as the American dream.

To hell with it.

I drove away. What was the point of staying there? I took Bay Shore, drove along the waterfront looking at all the houses, the mansions on the water all the way to the Ringling Museum. Was everyone who lived there a cheat, a criminal?

I made my way back through the North Trail, thinking about Tiffany. She had never been the answer to the mystery. She was just a poor girl who for some reason ran away from home and was picked up by Zavala. I couldn't imagine that old fuck having sex with her, with Maya, with kids. How many had there been, and where were they now?

And was it just sex, or was it more? His house was a museum of sexual artifacts. My imagination ran wild with images of what might have gone on behind those walls. I thought of Zoe. My hands clenched the steering wheel, my knuckles white with anger. It wasn't the children's fault—not Tiffany, not Maya. Would they ever learn to love without condition, without suspicion? The scars of abuse live forever. You don't recover from shit like that.

Maya might disappear forever, but she would never recover. What she suffered was not right. It wasn't fair to be young and exist only to please the whims of a man who manipulates, abuses, and tortures. I kept thinking of what Zavala had said about his sex shops. How it was the normal people in the suburbs who were his best customers. I passed the fancy houses along the wealthy Sapphire Shores neighborhood and wondered what kind of abuse might be happening behind the façade of the American dream.

Soon I found myself stuck on the south bridge to Siesta Key. It had opened for a huge sailboat. I sat in the traffic watching yet another rich motherfucker enjoying his wealth. Who needed a boat that size?

I drove down to Point of Rocks and parked under the sea grape tree. There was no activity in or outside the house. It was just as I had seen it the day before and before that.

Then a tow truck drove past real slow. It passed the house and kept going. It turned up ahead and came back and pulled up in front of the house. The driver got out, checked some papers, and walked to the front door and knocked.

He was a big guy. Bald. Had a smirk on his face like he knew more than the rest of us. And he probably did.

I watched him pace back and forth. He tried peeking into one of the shuttered windows. Then he scratched the back of his thick neck. He came back, checked the garage door, and looked around.

I got out of my car and crossed the street. "Can I help you?" I said.

He looked me up and down. "I'm looking for a Michael—" He glanced at the clipboard in his hand—"Boseman. Michael Boseman."

I nodded at the large house behind him. "That's his place."

"He around?"

I shrugged. "Haven't seen him in weeks."

He looked back at the house, at me, and scratched the side of his neck. "Who're you?"

I smiled. "I might ask you the same question."

He frowned. Looked pissed. Then he grinned. "You're not him, are you?"

I shook my head. "But I'm looking for him."

He laughed and rubbed his nose with the back of his hand. "You don't know where he's keeping his Jag, do you?"

"The car?"

He nodded and held up the clipboard for me to see. "I got a re-possession request from Sunfare Financing."

"No shit."

He smiled the way an accomplice might smile during a heist. I nodded in the direction of the house. "You check the garage?"

He looked back at the house and nodded. "I'll be back."

I can't say it didn't make me feel good to know Boseman was getting his eighty-five-thousand-dollar car repossessed. But it also set off an alarm: Boseman was broke. It hadn't occurred to me because of the house on the beach, the Jag. But the veil was torn off. If they were here for the car, maybe the house was next. Maybe it explained the empty house. The house, the car, it was just for appearances.

I sped home, thinking of what Petrillo had said about motive: money and love. Money. And. Love.

I went into my computer and tried to find information on Boseman's house. There was nothing under the County Appraiser's website—at least not under Boseman's name. But when I checked with Zillow I got a hit. The address was marked with a blue dot. Boseman's house was in pre-foreclosure.

I called Petrillo. "I have the motive. Boseman's broke."

"So what?"

"So, he was after Zavala's money."

"No one stole anything, Dexter. Nothing was missing from the house. Unless he's set up to inherit Zavala's millions, money doesn't figure into the equation."

My theory crumbled before my eyes. "Unless he was in on it with Maya. She's getting two million from the insurance. If those two are in it together, which is very likely . . ."

"It's a possibility," he said.

"And Joaquin del Pino is the executor of the official will."

"So I heard. We're getting warm."

"Yeah, but we still don't know who's inheriting the loot. Maybe you could have a word with him."

"Frey's on his way to meet him now."

I hung up and paced all over the house. My adrenaline was pumping. I needed a drink, something hard and cool. But I wanted to stay sober. I could see it all coming together. I hated to think that Maya was involved, but it made sense. It actually made me feel good that she had gotten some kind of revenge for what Zavala had done to her. But there was a small problem: If she and Boseman were in this together, who hired the goons that attacked me that night in Mexico?

* * *

About seven thirty that night I got a text from Petrillo: *meet at O'Leary's in half an hour.*

O'Leary's was the little Tiki bar and restaurant on the bay at the end of downtown. It was one of the best and only real tropical spots in Sarasota. The only drag was the food sucked. But the location made up for it.

It took me ten minutes to get there. I ordered a Red Stripe from the bar and sat on one of the tables looking out at the dark of the bay. The city lights gave off a red glow over the moored sailboats tilting from side to side with the tide, their rigging like tiny distant bells. The smell of salt and shitty fried food and coconut suntan lotion was all over the place. In the outdoor dining area, a man played guitar and sang a Bob Marley tune.

"Dexter." Petrillo came walking quickly. He placed his hand on my shoulder and sighed. "No dice."

Every ounce of energy escaped my veins. Petrillo ambled over to the bar, got himself a Corona, and came back to the table. "Del Pino says Zavala willed everything he owned to a number of charities for abused children and victims of sexual trafficking."

"All of it?"

"Every dime."

"Wait a minute. Del Pino has a charity for abused children. He's gonna make a killing out of the deal."

Petrillo drained half his beer in a single sip. He shook his head and pointed at me with the bottle. "No. That's why it took so long to figure out Zavala's will. Too many lawyers and too many nonprofits were involved. Everything had to be clear before they could announce it. Turns out Zavala didn't include del Pino's charity in the will at del Pino's own request. And he's donating his own fee to BRAVO."

"You're fucking kidding me."

"His words. Not mine."

"You think he's telling the truth?"

He laughed. "I'm a cop. He's a lawyer."

"Well, shit." I drank my beer. I went to the bar and got us another round. Then I got a text from Rachel: *where u?*

I answered: *O'Leary's. I'm buying.*

She texted back: *K*

I set the beers on the table and looked at the line of condos, their lights sparkling like diamonds. The Sarasota of the rich. The city of the Bosemans and the Zavalas.

Petrillo shoved me with his elbow. "Lighten up. You're taking it too personal."

I lowered my head, looked down at the table, the grain of the wood, the tracks the beer and food had left behind. "The thing is, I know there's something going on. I know there is." I glanced at Petrillo. "I can't say Boseman killed the guy for sure. But he's so fucking crooked. Why do they always get away with it?"

"They don't always. But sometimes, you just have to move on. You win some, you lose some."

I didn't want to believe him. But it was more than that. So long as the case remained open, I remained a suspect. I couldn't live with that shit.

I thought of Flor. I hoped to God she would find an axolotl. I needed something good to happen to restore my faith in humanity, in the system. In all of us. I bought another round at the bar. As I came back to the table, I saw Rachel walking quickly toward us. She didn't wait for me to put the beers down. She just hugged me, arms fully around my neck, hands pressing hard on my back, her face against the side of my neck.

I froze, feeling the heat and sweat coming off her body and pressing into mine.

"I'm sorry," she whispered.

"About what?"

She sobbed, but I knew she wasn't crying. "I am so sorry, Dex."

"Rachel . . ."

"Holly."

"What about her?" And then, just as she said her name again, it came to me in a flash with the two tiny syllables in her name: Hol-ly—the red lipstick on the glass in Boseman's poolside table, the butterfly sunglasses—the red VW beetle speeding out of Point of Rocks.

"Holly." She said it again. "I was parked across the street watching the house like you asked me. Then Holly drove up. She parked a little ahead of the house. She looked around. Got the mail and went inside. She was in there for about thirty minutes. Then she came back out, got into her car, and that was it."

"You sure?" I didn't want to believe it. Yet I knew it was true. Very fucking true. I had been an idiot for not seeing it before. She was breaking up with del Pino—because of Boseman?

She must have been with him the day I went to Boseman's house. She and Boseman had shaken up my place. They had taken my computer. They were after . . . Maya?

My knees weakened. Rachel held me, helped me to the table where Petrillo was looking at the boats, his knee bouncing to the rhythm of the guitar player in the dining area who was now belting out a mediocre rendition of "Margaritaville."

In those few seconds, everything about Holly, all my recent memories of her, raced past me like an old film. It had all been a setup: she appeared at Caragiulos when I was already looking for Maya. She showed up at my house immediately after it had been ransacked. She appeared after Petrillo and Frey did a number on me. She was there after I came back from Mexico. She wanted information. She wanted to know where I was with my investigation, to know how safe she and Boseman were, to know what the cops knew.

"Motherfuckers."

Rachel rubbed my back. "Easy, Dex."

Petrillo took one of the beers I put on the table. "What's up?"

Rachel told him. She explained everything while I stared at the sailboats bobbing in the water, getting seasick. My stomach cramped with jealousy and anger and betrayal—all hope doused with diesel and set on fire.

I downed my beer and slammed the bottle on the table.

Petrillo grabbed my wrist. "Easy, Vega."

I tore away from his grip. "It's all yours now, right?"

Rachel took my arm. "Dex."

I backed away from Petrillo. "You know what to do, right?"

I turned away. Rachel and I went to the bar. I ordered tequila. I took them in shots like a frat boy at a rush party. I wanted to get the fuck out of my mind.

CHAPTER TWENTY-THREE

My bender lasted four days. It was a blur that left no memory. I escaped like I always did. But eventually I had to come back. And I did on a Saturday morning, four days after Rachel had given me the news about Holly.

I opened my eyes. My head pounded at the temples. My mouth was raw and dry as if I'd shoved a fistful of sand into it.

A tropical storm blew outside, making a racket on the tin roof. I stumbled out of bed. Poured a glass of water from the faucet and drank like it was life. I knew I would need a hair of the dog, but it was the first time in days that my surroundings appeared clear. I had to stop. I knew that. But I wasn't sure I could. Or that I even wanted to. I popped open a Corona, squeezed a lime in it, added shots of Tabasco sauce, took long, sour sips.

It burned my lips. Leveled me off.

Rachel was lying on the couch reading a book with Mimi curled up at her side. When I shuffled out, she set the book down and smiled. "Well, good morning, sunshine!"

I made it to the chair on the other side of the coffee table. I took another sip of beer and set it down. "What's going on?"

She sat up. "You tell me." Mimi hopped off the couch, stretched, and walked slowly to her place by the window.

I shook my head. "I think the worst is over."

"You're funny when you're drunk."

"Was I bad?"

"If I were you, I wouldn't go back to Caragiulos."

"You were with me all this time?"

"What can I say?" She leaned forward and grabbed my beer and took a long drink. "You were buying."

"Rachel, I'm sorry."

"Put it out of your mind like everything else. If you can't see it, it doesn't exist."

"Come on."

"You're an escape artist, Dexter. You're real good at eluding your problems."

"Please." I raised my hand. "Spare me."

She stood. "No. I won't spare you a damn thing." She stepped around the coffee table and leaned over me. "You can be a real piece of shit, you know that?"

"I'm sorry. I was drunk."

"It's not about what you did when you were in your drunken bender. It's that you went on one. That you couldn't stand up and face the fact that Holly isn't perfect."

"I loved her."

"No you didn't. You put her on a pedestal and worshiped who you thought she was. You've been lying to yourself all this time. You just refuse to admit it. Fuck you."

"Jesus, Rachel."

"Come on, Dex. Open your eyes."

Her lower lip trembled. I had never seen her so emotional. I spread my arms. "I didn't know . . ."

"Well, now you do. But what's worse is that you're a fucking coward." She waved, looked away for a moment, then pointed her index finger at me like it was a gun. "Man, you talk tough. You're all fuck this and fuck that, but you're so goddamn scared, you can't face your problems."

I looked at the beer.

"No," she said. "I'm not talking about the booze. We all do that. I'm talking about standing up for the shit you always say you stand for. When the shit hits the fan, you run away and hide in the booze."

At that instant I felt my head pop. It was as if someone had slapped the back of my neck and raised the curtain. I saw the farce of my life crumbling like Boseman's nonexistent fortune. Rachel was right. When things got tough for me, I bailed. I ran as far away from my problems as I could. I did it when that cop shot my father, when I left for college in Houston, during my divorce, when the paper laid me off. All these years I'd been running away.

I dropped my head in my hands and closed my eyes, shut them as tight as I could. Rachel sat on the armrest and put her arm around my shoulder. "Life ain't easy, is it?" She rocked me back and forth. "When I came out of the closet, I learned about it the hard way. But you can't run away all the time. Your problems won't go away if you don't face them. You just have to face the fact that the world is not perfect."

"And that people are assholes," I said.

She laughed. "And that people are assholes."

"Especially lawyers and preppy women who think they want to do good, but really just want to be rich."

"Especially them bitches."

I laughed and we hugged. Just being friends with Rachel made me the luckiest man alive.

"So what's the latest?" I said.

Rachel grabbed the beer and took a long swig. Then she sat back on the couch, the whole time her eyes on me as if she were trying to read what my deal was.

"You sure you want to know?" she said.

I nodded.

"Petrillo called last night. Holly won't say a peep, except that she's innocent. But Petrillo put the Mexican cops on it and they arrested Boseman pretty damn quick, if you can believe that."

I laughed. "I'll believe it when I see it."

"Well, they did. Petrillo said they got the juice out of him. He was blackmailing Zavala because he knew what Zavala was doing to the girls."

"Because Boseman had dated Maya."

She passed me the beer. "It tastes pretty good. A little too spicy for me."

I nodded. "It's an ancient Mexican hangover cure."

She smiled. "But Petrillo doesn't think he killed Zavala."

"I kind of had that figured."

"Shit. Aren't you the fucking detective."

"Petrillo said it. No motive."

"Anyway, you were right. Boseman was broke. When Zavala was killed, he and Holly went after you to see if you had any leads on Maya. They knew she was getting the insurance money so they were trying to blackmail her. They figured they could get money from her by threatening to drag her into the mess and pinning Zavala's murder on her."

"So that's why Boseman was in Mexico."

"That's what Petrillo said."

"Did he get to Maya?"

"Apparently not. They're holding him, waiting for the paperwork and all that shit."

"And Holly?"

"You really want to know?"

"I have to deal with it, right?"

"She's at county without bail. She says she's innocent, but Boseman already ratted her out. Petrillo's waiting until they get Boseman in so they can look at the whole picture."

"Fuck."

I felt terrible for Holly. But I felt pretty bad for myself. Not sorry, just shitty, like something had been stolen from me. And yet, everything was the same. And the fact was, I never had Holly. Even in the early days when we were together, there was an invisible wall. The other night was the same. And I think I realized that then, but like Rachel said, I just looked the other way because I didn't want to deal with the truth. I could only blame myself.

The rain let up some. I stood and walked over to the shelves of records. Today was a Van Morrison kind of day. "So if Boseman and Holly didn't kill Zavala, who did?"

Rachel shrugged. "Who knows?"

I put the record on. *Astral Weeks*. The original Warner Brother's Seven Artist release. Sublime.

"You know what I need," I said. "A vacation."

"You?"

We laughed. I stretched and shuffled into the kitchen and started on breakfast. I called out to Rachel: "Eggs, hot dogs, and Sriracha?"

* * *

It took me a couple of days to recover from the hangover and clear out the nasty blur that had clouded most of my week. Things finally began to feel normal. There was no way I could erase Holly from my consciousness. I couldn't just rub her out like she never existed. But now she was just a person in my past. A sad memory.

I read in the newspaper, in an article by the brilliant Jason Kirkpatrick, that Holly and Boseman were being charged with two counts of extortion. Court date for arraignment had been set up for late November. Del Pino was preparing to auction off Zavala's property. The artwork, it turned out, was as real as art can be. There was a lot of talk that it would fetch millions. Three members of the board of the Ringling Museum of Art and a county comptroller and the State Attorney's office were going to monitor how the money would be distributed to the different nonprofits Zavala had included in his will. There were a number of them and they were all local: one helped needy children, another operated a shelter for runaways and abused children. There was another that helped sexual trafficking victims, and a women's shelter. True to his word, del Pino stepped away from the proceedings and was quoted in an article in *Sara-Scene Magazine* that he would be donating his fee to his own charity. I was surprised. Joaquin del Pino's behavior through this whole thing restored my confidence in people.

And still, I could not reconcile with the fact that no one had caught Zavala's killer. I began to suspect that Maya had done it. That she had come back to Sarasota from Mexico, killed her abuser, and then gone back to Mexico before disappearing forever into a new life. And maybe Boseman knew it. Maybe that was what he had on her.

I couldn't blame her. If I was right about that, I would be satisfied. But I was not convinced. I couldn't see a person like her, so poised and understanding of her own situation, bludgeoning a man with a giant penis. I saw no violence in her whatsoever.

But then there were Rachel's words: I put women on a pedestal; I think of them the way I imagine them to be. So maybe I was way off about Maya being incapable of murder. Perhaps, under the proper circumstances, we all are. But I would never know the truth about Maya.

I tried to get back to work. I sent out e-mails and story ideas to *Sarasota City Magazine*, but the editor said I sucked at writing about designer homes and real estate. She said we needed to think of something more serious, something with meat on it but not too heavy. "Our readers don't like bad news," she said. "We're a lifestyle magazine."

I swallowed my pride and contacted my old paper. The *Sarasota Herald* had hired a few young reporters, recent graduates who had replaced me and the other older reporters. I laughed. I wasn't even forty years old and I was old. I couldn't believe it.

Still, the city editor suggested I keep in touch, e-mail story ideas. "We pay a hundred per story," she said. She even sounded proud about that. I did the math in my head. I would have to write ten stories a week to make a livable wage. All I could do was shake my head and put on a record that offered hope: Bruce Springsteen's *Born to Run*.

I sat down at my computer and took a big leap. I e-mailed the big guys. I tried them all: The *Washington Post*, The *LA Times*, *New York Times*, *Time*, *Men's Journal*, *Travel and Leisure*, *Forbes*. I pitched over thirty newspapers and magazines a whole slew of story ideas: travel stories, investigative pieces, features. I offered them my services in case they needed anything in the area. I told them I was willing to travel. Whatever they wanted. I even suggested a story to *Smithsonian Magazine* about Flor's quixotic search for the axolotl.

Just the fact that there were so many publications I could pitch gave me hope in a business I thought was extinct. I had no qualms about receiving rejections. Most editors didn't even bother to write back. A few were polite. Still, I knew there was a place for me out there. I knew eventually I would be back to doing what I did well.

I had hope.

But I won't lie. I still had this buzzing in the back of my head about Nick Zavala's murder. I hated the fact that someone had killed a man and was walking away free. I think that what bothered me most was the motivation. Who had done this, and why?

Every few days I drove past Zavala's old house on Bay Shore and then did a little tour up and down the North Trail. I'm not sure what I was looking for, or if I was even looking for someone or something. I kept thinking of Tiffany. Child Services could have placed her in a foster home or a shelter. I wanted to know she was okay. I checked with some of the shelters and advocacy groups, but these things are confidential. Their job is to protect the victims even from their own family. I followed up with Petrillo, but he knew nothing. It was as if she had vanished from the planet.

Then, on a rainy Thursday afternoon I received an e-mail from Flor. She had found the axolotl. Two, actually. She was ecstatic. She said it opened the possibility for more funding for her group to expand the search. But more important, she was validated. All those months swimming in dirty canals had paid off.

I did a Google search and found articles in the Mexican newspapers. *Reforma* had a great photograph of the team on location in Xochimilco. Flor looked as if she'd just come out of the water. Her smile was radiant. Her hair was a mess, but a beautiful mess that reminded me of our nights together in her apartment.

For the first time since I'd been back, I realized how much I missed her. I read every article I could find about the discovery of the two axolotls. I had no idea two salamanders, two ugly little reptiles, would be such a big deal. But the Mexican press was going to town with the story. Thanks to Flor's hard work, the little animal and its habitat would be protected.

I looked at the brighter side of things. The axolotl was not extinct. Journalism was not extinct. And humanity, the good guys, were not extinct. Del Pino and even Petrillo demonstrated that. Not to mention Rachel.

Late that same afternoon I got an e-mail from *Smithsonian Magazine*. They were interested in the axolotl story. Could I get started right away. They offered a decent day-rate plus expenses. I was going to Mexico. I was going to see Flor.

Hope was not extinct.

On a wet Sunday afternoon, I went to West Marine to buy snorkeling gear. A mask and snorkel and a pair of flippers. I wanted to be able to dive into the canals with Flor. I wanted to know what she had been seeing, what she had been living all these months.

On my way to the checkout, I saw a young woman I vaguely recognized. She was with an older man and they were looking at a bin of discount watches near the checkout. She picked one up and showed it to the man. "How about this one?" she asked.

I advanced to the register and saw the side of her face. Tiffany.

My heart stopped. I wanted to reach out, ask her if she was okay, if she was aware of what had happened with Boseman and Holly. If she knew who had killed Zavala. But I was paralyzed with fear. It was like seeing a ghost. And I guess it would be like opening another chapter that shouldn't be opened.

"Forty-seven fifty." The cashier's voice brought me out of my trance. I slid my credit card into the machine. But I couldn't take my eyes off Tiffany.

"Come on, Dad," she said and pulled the man by the arm. At the end of the bin she picked up another watch and looked at it. Then her eyes met mine and they locked into place like a target. It was only a second, but it felt like hours. Then she looked down and dropped the watch and picked up another.

"Sir?" Once again the cashier brought me back to the store. She pointed to the little credit card machine in front of me. "Credit or debit?"

I punched the credit button, then the green one, accepting the total. I looked back up. Tiffany had put on a watch and was holding it up for her father to see. I thought she looked good. Certainly better than when I had seen her outside Zavala's house.

"Please, Dad?" Her voice was sweet, full of innocence.

I took my receipt and walked to the door. But before I left, I turned. Tiffany had her back to me now. The man, her father, was smiling and holding up a different watch. Then he turned slightly and dropped his smile. He was the man who had been beating Zavala outside Memories Lounge. He didn't look as ragged as he had that night. But his eyes were the same color as Tiffany's—they had the same spark, the same attitude.

Just before I turned away, I noticed the pendant hanging from his neck. It was an oval medallion. It had a man on a horse killing a dragon. St. George. Gold surrounded by tiny little red rubies. But the side had lost a piece, as if someone had taken a bite out of it. Or a bullet had nicked it on the side.

When I looked at him again, he was staring at me. Smiling.

I walked away, across the electronic doors and into the parking lot. I got in my old Subaru and drove north on the Trail. When I got to a red light, I dialed my ex-wife on my cell phone and asked her to put Zoe on. "I have a lot to tell her," I said.